FRANCESCA
and the
MAGIC BIKE

FRANCESCA
and the
MAGIC BIKE

CYNTHIA NUGENT

RAINCOAST BOOKS

Vancouver

Raincoast Books acknowledges the ongoing financial support of the Government of Canada through The Canada Council for the Arts and the Book Publishing Industry Development Program (BPIDP); and the Government of British Columbia through the BC Arts Council.

Editor: Lynn Henry
Cover design: Tannice Goddard
Interior design: Tannice Goddard

CANADIAN CATALOGUING IN PUBLICATION DATA

Nugent, Cynthia, 1954–
Francesca and the magic bike / Cynthia Nugent.

ISBN 1-55192-561-3

I. Title.

PS8627.U34F73 2004   JC813 .6   C2004-901956-2

Library of Congress Control Number: 2004 092419

Raincoast Books   In the United States:
9050 Shaughnessy Street   Publishers Group West
Vancouver, British Columbia   1700 Fourth Street
Canada, V6P 6E5   Berkeley, California
www.raincoast.com   94710

At Raincoast Books we are committed to protecting the environment and to the responsible use of natural resources. We are acting on this commitment by working with suppliers and printers to phase out our use of paper produced from ancient forests. This book is one step towards that goal. It is printed on 100% ancient-forest-free paper (40% post-consumer recycled), processed chlorine- and acid-free, and supplied by New Leaf paper. It is printed with vegetable-based inks. For further information, visit our website at www.raincoast.com. We are working with Markets Initiative (www.oldgrowthfree.com) on this project.

Printed in Canada by Webcom Ltd.

10 9 8 7 6 5 4 3 2 1

For I. M. Birtwistle,
patron saint of artists
and my very own Augusta.

Chapter One

It could have been a witch's house on that narrow forgotten street at the edge of downtown. Or maybe the house of the lady-with-a-hundred-cats, the one who shuffled home each day laden with shopping bags to meet eager, straight-tailed mewing.

In the overgrown front hedge was a dark opening. Hanging off one hinge and wedged against the walk, an iron gate led to ragged bushes and worn front steps. A quartet of cats flicked past the broken banisters or stared unblinkingly from the darkest recesses of the porch.

Virginia creeper clung with shrivelled brown hands to the brickwork of the narrow, falling-down house. Holding it up on either side like a pair of crutches were two tall cedars dusted with snow. Slivers of light gleamed through the dark branches from a top floor window.

Everywhere creatures made their nests: pigeons in the eaves, a family of raccoons in the unusable chimney, mice multiplied in the garden shed and a skunk combed back dirt with long claws to nibble thoughtfully on sowbugs behind the broken lattices under the porch.

Suddenly the front door opened, spilling out amber through a crack just large enough for a cat to scoot in. He slid unnoticed around the stout ankles of Mrs. Violet Slatternly. She was dressed in coat and hat, her hand on the door handle, about to call up the stairs. The cat slipped silently into the dark corner behind the stairwell, blinked once, then waited.

"I'll be off then, Missus H," Mrs. Slatternly called, glancing down at another feline face trying to squeeze in through the narrow opening. She pushed the door closed, forcing the cat backwards. There was a protesting meow from the other side.

"Already?" A voice leapt down the stairs. "And what time do you make it, Mrs. Slatternly?"

"Nearly five, missus."

"Extraordinary what you call 'nearly.' I make it 4:25. Whatever do I pay you for?"

Violet sighed and put down her bag.

"Oh go on," said the voice. "I'll expect you thirty-five minutes early tomorrow."

"Yes, Missus H." The housekeeper picked up her bag and turned to the door.

"Have you put out Dan's dinner and fed the cats?"

"Done."

"The kettle filled?"

"To the brim, Missus H."

"How many times do I have to tell you? Not to the top. You know I can't manage it when it's full. Three-quarters, three-quarters full. I've told you time and again."

Violet put down her bag again and clomped to the kitchen to slop some water out of the kettle. "Anything else, Missus H?" she called up, the courtesy strangling on its way out through her clenched throat.

"Well, I hope you've left me something to eat. I know there's not much of me left, but I still need something to keep body and soul together."

"A nice cheese-and-tomato sandwich and some vanilla pudding with fruit cocktail for afters."

"What luxury! What culinary excess! I shall die of gluttony. Oh, go on then. And don't forget to go to the butcher's tomorrow morning. You've got the cheque?"

"Yes, Missus H. I won't, Missus H. Night, Missus H." And not waiting for a reply, Violet Slatternly banged out the door and grumbled down the front steps, shoving cats out of the way all the way down. "Thinks she's the blinking queen. Ringing and ringing her little bell. One of these days she'll ring that bell and Violet Slatternly won't be there to climb those blinking stairs one more blinking time."

Inside, the cat slid out from the dark stairwell and with tail erect, flowed through the gloom, up the narrow staircase covered with a threadbare runner held in place by tarnished stair rails, and across a small landing where minute, over-varnished, dark paintings lost in mammoth frames tilted above a low shelf crammed with books and knickknacks. Up and up he went, to finally peer into the fantastical bedroom of Augusta Halberton-Ffrench.

"Who's there?" The old lady's head turned sharply and her dark glasses caught the dancing lights of the chandelier above her bed.

"Meow."

"Oh, it's you, Harold. Mrs. Slatternly was supposed to have put you out for the night. Otherwise, falling over a cat could be the death of me. Dan here knows how to stay out of the way of an old blind lady, don't you Danny Boy?" Dan's tail thumped on the floor. Harold leapt onto her lap and she stroked him. "Well, just this once, seeing as it's you."

Later, Augusta felt her way downstairs and along the hallway to the kitchen, extra mindful of the possibility of Harold being underfoot. She found a tea-towel-covered plate on the counter. She switched on the kettle and listened for it to boil. Using both hands to steady the surrounding cups, she lifted a cup off of its hook, then felt carefully along the counter for the teabags.

"Drat that woman! I tell her and tell her to put things back where they belong. How am I supposed to find anything if she doesn't? Why can't people listen?" Impatiently, Augusta swept her hand in ever-widening arcs over the cluttered counter. Her hand connected with an object and before she could stop it, it sailed off the edge, clanging when it hit the floor.

"Violet Slatternly, you have the mind of a flea!"

Holding onto the edge of the counter, Augusta carefully lowered herself, groping downwards from drawer handle to cupboard handle until she was on her knees on the floor. She could feel spilled teabags everywhere. She found the tin but the lid had rolled away to Lord knows where.

Crouching, she collected the bags into the tin, then felt up as high as she could to replace it on the counter, before using both hands to haul herself up again.

She listened to the news on the kitchen radio while she stood at the counter eating her sandwich and drinking her tea. "I don't believe it!" she remarked several times during the course of the broadcast, disgusted with the state of the world. She took a pill from each of the many bottles lined up on the counter, and two from the bottle with a homemade knob of masking tape on the lid. "Why I bother to stay alive, I don't know." After swallowing her medicine, she felt her way out along the walls to the front door to check the lock before climbing the stairs to the bedroom again. Dan shuffled a few feet behind, slowly wagging his tail. Augusta paused halfway up on the small landing to listen to the sound of a Hammond organ coming from next door. Only a narrow gravel-lined space separated the stained-glass oriole on the landing of Augusta's house from the air duct of the house next door.

"Listen to him, Dan. Drunk again."

"*Hit the road, Jack, and don't you come back no more, no more ...*" came the raucous imitation of Ray Charles from the neighbour's air duct. Then the music abruptly stopped and the strident voice turned into a whimper, "Oh, Cally ..."

Augusta started up the stairs again, muttering, "Ronald Rudderless, you are a fool. Cally left you years ago. Pull yourself together."

Early the next morning, as Mrs. Slatternly laboured up the stairs with Augusta's first cup of tea, a small girl sat in the front seat of a Greyhound bus. Her tangled red hair dazzled softly in the pale winter sunshine. Instead of watching the scenery rush by, she was carefully cutting out a small blue illustration of a bus from the front of a scheduling pamphlet using a pair of yellow-handled children's scissors. She uncapped her red gluestick and rubbed the back of the bus-shaped piece of paper, then patiently pressed it into the scrapbook spread across her knees. Then, with pencil poised, she called to the driver, "Any bumps coming?"

"No, but there'll be a tunnel in five minutes."

She nodded to herself, then pencilled: "This is the bus I rode to meet my Father for the first time."

On the same page was a photo of a grey cat sitting up and looking straight into the camera. Underneath it she'd written, "Pickles. My Best Friend." There was also a picture of a pale smiling woman in pajamas sitting cross-legged on a hospital bed. The woman wore a baseball cap and, if you looked closely, you could see a white medical bracelet on her thin wrist. The caption read: "Mommy with no hair."

The girl gently stroked the photo.

Chapter Two

Ron Rudderless woke up with a headache. While he shaved his round face, he looked in the mirror at his frightening ginger hair sticking out at every possible angle. The razor shook in his hand.

"I WILL be a good father. I will BE a good father. I will be a GOOD FATHER!" he repeated to his soapy face. He pushed up his nose to shave underneath. It gave him a decidedly piggy appearance.

"Oink, oink," he giggled, which made his head hurt. "Oops, no laughing." Sighing, he stuck bits of tissue on his assorted bleeding nicks. Then he tottered down the hall to the kitchen and threw his arms open to an imaginary audience. "Hey there, ladies and germs! What did the baby light bulb say to the daddy light bulb? ... I wuv you watts and watts. TA DA!" Muttering "Applause applause," he bowed to the fridge and the stove.

"Now, breakfast, breakfast ... What'll it be? Something healthy. A new start." He opened the fridge.

"Gaak! Pee yew!" He slammed the door in horror. "Make a note: shopping." Then, brightening, he cried, "I know, I'll eat out! It's a special day. It's ... The Day of the Daughter!"

Grabbing his coat and scarf, Ron Rudderless ran out the door singing, "Oh what a beautiful morning ... Ouch, that hurts."

Normally, Ron took the streetcar to work to reduce the risk of being stopped for impaired driving while weaving home at night. His battered leather briefcase contained nothing but a bottle of gin and a ukulele. At work, in his claustrophobic, dusty office in the basement of City Hall, he put the bottle in a drawer. In the long hours between issuing licenses to long-haired street musicians and vendors of beaded bracelets and zodiac earrings, he'd pull down the green blind on the door by its yellowing tassel and take out a smudged glass. Then he'd sing softly while he strummed on the ukulele, daydreaming of his musical career taking off again and Cally returning to his open arms.

Ron had moved back to his hometown soon after his ex-wife, Cally, ran off with an electric guitar player, aptly stagenamed "the Menace." None of them knew then that she had dashed after romance while pregnant with Ron's child.

For a few years, Ron and his elderly mother had muddled on together. He spoke little and would sing

"Bumpety bump bump" to the tune of "Shave and a Haircut" when an answer was expected of him. His mother just looked at him in exasperation and told him to take out the garbage, or to make himself useful and put on the kettle. When she died, he inherited the house. As the years passed the house grew darker and more ramshackle. He filled it with broken musical instruments that he picked up at junk sales, intending to repair them and sell them for a profit. Then one day, nearly eleven years after he'd moved home, he got a short scrawled letter from Cally saying that she had cancer. And then, just as suddenly, the phone rang and a woman said Cally had died. Ron continued to hold the receiver to his ear but grief blotted out everything. Then he realized the voice was still talking.

"... I've been taking care of your daughter. Cally said if anything bad happened to call you."

Ron shook his head. "You must be mistaken. I don't have a daughter."

"Yes, yes. Cally said you are Francesca's father. Most definitely."

Ron was having difficulty thinking. He tried to focus. "How old ...?"

"Nearly ten-years-old. Cally said to tell you red hair like you. Cally said you would be a good daddy."

Ron sat down with a thump. The woman continued, "That Menace person ..." She drew in her breath sharply and muttered angrily in Chinese. "That Menace individual is sending her to you on the bus. Long way for little girl. She will be there next Friday at 3:00 p.m. in the afternoon. I am sorry to telephone with bad news."

Ron said, "I'm sorry, please tell me your name again?"

"Margaret Chow. Cally was my good neighbour. I liked her very much." The woman started to cry.

Ron's heart was overloaded. He had loved Cally so much. And to find out after all these years that he had a daughter. It was too much. He got drunk for a week. He left work early or was late, or didn't show up at all, which resulted in him receiving his second letter of warning from work. One more and he'd be unemployed.

But this particular Friday, Ron was determined to be a Good Father. He left his bottle in the drawer except for a little nip in the morning and another little nip at lunch. Still, by the time he walked into the noisy diesel-fume filled hangar of the bus station, his fragile good mood had deserted him. His head ached and one eye was twitching. He felt like he was about to be executed — there would be no turning back.

He was early for the bus, so he went to the coffee shop. He browsed the news stand. He double-checked the arrival time with the bored clerk at the ticket booth. How could the man be so indifferent on such a momentous day? He spent the last half hour standing in the arrivals area. The bus was late. He looked up to read the sign again. He was in the wrong bay! Oh no! He didn't want his daughter getting off the bus with no one to meet her. He tore around the huge concrete arrivals area staring frantically at every sign. Gasping, he staggered up to the correct bay just as the bus wheeled in. That must be her, right up front: his ten-year-old daughter Francesca. Ron halted, paralyzed with shock. "I don't think I'm up to this," he thought wildly. But there she was, jumping off the last step of the bus wearing a backpack and a parka and carrying a big book in her arms. On her head she wore a multicoloured knitted Peruvian toque with the earflaps turned up and ties dangling.

Confused, she stopped dead in front of the bus door, causing a disgruntled pileup.

"Move, kid!" someone said.

"Step aside, please," the driver called. "Yes, you!" He poked the girl, who leapt, half-twirled and hopped out of the way as if the concrete was covered with hopscotch squares. Tired, irritated passengers shoved past. Anxiously, Ron hurried forward as his daughter disappeared around the corner of the bus. She was following the driver, who had opened the sides of the vehicle and was pulling out luggage. Slight as a water bug and just as comical, she skipped and hopped back and forth, trying to keep out of everyone's way. Looking at his daughter, Ron felt shy love well up inside him along with the feeling that he didn't deserve her.

Then she saw him. Her eyes widened with recognition and she skittered over.

Wide green-grey eyes stared up at Ron. The toque stood straight up on the girl's head and pointed elfin ears struck out from bursts of copper hair. She had a determined chin and a nose like a blob of pink plasticine.

"Francesca?" It was a dumb question. This was indisputably her.

The child now stared at Ron's galoshes. Their unzipped rubber sides hung down as if exhausted. On the way up, her eyes took in his grey overcoat and brown cardigan that failed to button over a green plaid stomach. His face was round and his rust-coloured hair stood out in tufts.

"Are you my Dad?"

"None other." Ron attempted joviality. Francesca continued to stare. In her hand was a grubby envelope with his name on it.

"May I?" Ron said, reaching gingerly for the letter.

"Go on." The bus driver appeared from around the side of the bus and put down a cardboard suitcase. "You might as well. Everyone else on the bus has read it." While Ron unfolded the letter the bus driver went on, "I've kept my eye on her for the last eighteen hours. She's a handful, that one." He stared at Ron expectantly as if awaiting his reward. When Ron didn't answer, he turned back to the luggage grumbling, "Babysitting certainly isn't in my job description."

But Ron didn't notice; he was reading the note:

Hey Man,

Can't get my head around taking care of a kid. I'm touring nonstop these days and heard you ain't giggin' no more. I know Cally would want her to be with you because she's your kid. Maybe Cally left you for me because you weren't going places musically, but hey! that'll probably make you a great dad, right? Remember the old days, man? That band was swingin'. Keep blowin' your horn (or not as the case may be).

Merv (the Menace) Murphy
P.S. Don't mention the cat.

Ron stuffed the letter into his pocket and smiled at Francesca. He picked up her cardboard suitcase and said, "The car's over here." He took her hand, awed at his audacity, noting its smallness in a secret rush of joy and amazement, and led her to his beat-up Toyota. He opened the passenger door. Francesca gawked at the fast food wrappers on the floor and the old stinky blanket on the torn seat. It had a partially eaten pizza on it. Ron tossed the pizza box into the back, thinking the car *did* look bad. He hadn't noticed before. How long had that graffiti been on the door?

"Look at all this garbage. Boy, are you a pig!" Francesca exclaimed.

"Bumpety bump bump," Ron mumbled, blushing. "Only temporary." He couldn't think of anything else to say.

"You don't talk much," she said, as they got in and drove out of the parking lot.

"Bumpety bump bump," Ron sang again and grinned and winked as if that meant something.

Frankie squinted at him. "The Menace says you're a musician too. Mom says musicians are all idle and useless."

Startled, Ron glanced down at the child. She was so small she could barely see over the dashboard. He signaled for a left turn.

"Um. Well. I work in an office now, issuing busking licenses to street musicians for the city. You could say I'm still in the music business — sort of an impresario of the sidewalk. Heh heh." He smiled down at her, pleased with his little joke. She frowned back at him.

"Hey, don't judge me by the Menace," pleaded Ron.

"Electric guitar players are known bad apples — very unreliable and stuck on themselves. Drummers and trumpet players are the same. Terrible bunch. I'm a euphonium player — like a little tuba," he explained, noticing her puckered eyebrows. "Euphonium players are sensitive and kind, and much more intelligent than trombone players. Trombone players are as thick as planks. You wouldn't want a father who was a trombone player. But I'm not *too* sensitive and poetic — not like flute players. They're so sensitive they'll burst into tears if you look at them."

Ron stopped talking, amazed at himself. He hadn't said so much at one time in years. He thought Francesca looked impressed. Then she said, "You have throw-up stuck to your shoulder."

Ron gave his shoulder a quick check. Oh dear. He remembered he'd briefly fallen asleep in the front seat of the car last night. Evidently he'd landed on the unfinished pizza he'd bought after spending the evening in the bar. A gluey hunk of cheese and olives was adhered to his coat. "Oh. That's pizza. I was saving it for later," he explained lightly, and he peeled off the hunk and stuck it in his mouth. "Which reminds me. We should stop at the grocery store. What do you like to eat?"

Francesca leaned back stiffly in her padded coat so she could look Ron in the face. Her mouth opened in horror. Then she folded one mittened hand over the other and said, "I don't like asparagus. I don't like Brussels sprouts. I don't like escargot or chicken livers or shrimp cocktail. And I don't like pizza stuck to coats."

In the supermarket, Ron and Francesca raced a shopping

cart up and down every aisle. Ron took one of everything she pointed at: a box of sugar-frosted cereal; prewrapped lunch-size packets of peanut butter and crackers; an aerosol can of cheese; canned pasta shaped like dinosaurs; frozen mini-pizzas; individual boxes of fruit punch; granola bars; dried fruit in rubbery strips; canned chicken-noodle soup; and white bread. He got himself canned beans, sausages, eggs, bologna, milk for tea, and a half pound of butter. He felt proud of himself like a real provider, until he was paying the cashier and Francesca cried, "We forgot cat food!"

"But, but, Francesca," Ron stuttered, "... we haven't got a cat."

"Yes, we do. We've got Pickles. The Menace sent Pickles by special animal courier two weeks ago."

Suddenly Ron remembered the "PS" in the note. "Menace, you always were a jerk," he muttered under his breath. Out loud, he said, "Oh, of course. Pickles." They left their shopping cart with the cashier and ran back to the aisles so that Francesca could pick out Pickles' favourite food.

Ron heaved the groceries and Francesca into the car, and ran around to leap into the driver's seat. He started the engine with a roar. All the way home he wore the pained grin of a man showing his teeth to a dentist. He just knew that the Menace had got rid of the cat. Menace was too lazy and cheap to arrange for a crate and transport for Pickles.

"Haven't you noticed how smart Pickles is?" asked Francesca.

"Bumpety bump bump," sang Ron.

Francesca stared at him askance but persisted. "Pickles can fetch like a dog. She runs after crumpled paper and brings it back. And she can catch mice. You'll never have another mouse. Once a mouse ate the corners out of every single box and bag in our cupboard. There were big holes. You could see the little nibbles. It ate the rice — raw rice! And two boxes of cereal, white sugar, and lots and lots of flour. And there were little mouse poos everywhere."

"Sounds like an army of mice," Ron replied, grateful for something noncommittal to say.

"But Pickles got him, like that!" Francesca tried to snap her fingers.

"Like that!" said Ron, snapping.

"Yeah! Pickles sits on the table and pushes stuff off one by one. She looks over the edge each time to see it fall. It's so funny. Has she done that yet at your house?"

"Bumpety bump," muttered Ron, swerving left.

"She sits in the sink and tries to eat the water drops as they fall out of the tap. She always sleeps in my bed with me and wakes me up in the morning by licking my face. Her tongue is really rough. She only sleeps with me. She knows when I'm sad and curls up on my lap. Like when Mom ..."

Ron looked over quickly. Francesca had stopped talking and was rubbing a circle on the cold grubby window with her finger. A few minutes later she said, "Pickles is the only one who knows how I feel. She's my best friend. We've been together my whole life."

Ron felt sick.

They pulled up in front of an old house with a month's worth of sodden flyers on the front porch. Francesca stood on the sidewalk staring at it while Ron unloaded the car. He slammed the trunk, hurried her into the house and dumped everything on the kitchen table.

The kitchen was cold, gloomy and large, with tall cupboards and counters, gas stove and the rounded hulk of an antique fridge. In the centre of the room, a round turquoise table with chrome trim was orbited by the white stars and red-ringed planets on the worn black linoleum. Francesca walked across the kitchen floor. It was like walking across the universe. She peered through a doorway into a room full of dressers, boxes, a heaped collection of old Bakelite radios, a prehistoric electric organ, and piles and piles of junk. Ron followed her anxiously. He turned on the light. "This was my mother's room. You can have it now."

Francesca stood in the doorway surveying the congestion of her father's collection of broken musical instruments and old console radios. He waved his hands at the tarnished brass horns and hubcaps full of radio dials.

"My little sideline in music for the masses. Repair and resale. I was just about to start working on them when you arrived," he grunted as he cleared a space for Francesca on the chesterfield behind the dust-covered Hammond organ.

"I'll get some sheets and blankets and a pillow." He pulled out the middle drawer of the tall oak dresser. It was full of a clattering accumulation of horn valves and clarinet keys. He dumped the whole mess into the bottom drawer. Then he tipped the contents of Francesca's cardboard suitcase into the middle drawer. "We'll move a bed into here later."

But Francesca had left the room and was looking under tables and behind chairs. "Pickles, Pickles!" she called.

Ron's heart lurched. "I have to make a phone call," he said. "I'll be right back." He ran up the stairs to his bedroom and closed the door. He dialed the Menace with trembling hands.

"Hey. You're on," announced the unmistakably self-satisfied voice of Merv the Menace Murphy.

"Menace, this is Ron Rudderless. Where's Pickles?"

"Oh man. That cat's dead."

"Dead! Are you sure? Maybe it ran away."

"Nah. It got run over by a truck."

"Oh God. Couldn't you have told her? Had a little cat funeral or something?"

"No way. That feline was squashed flat as pancake."

"Why didn't you get her another cat?"

"Are you kidding? I hate cats. Man, I was jumping for joy when that cat died."

"So you told her you sent it to *me*. That is so low. Look Menace, I want you to tell her the truth right now." Ron was sweating. Dread gnawed in his stomach like a rat.

"No way, I'm outta the loop now, Big R. You're the dad. You tell her. It's your gig now. Hey, and Ron?"

"What?" asked Ron miserably.

"Don't call me no more. We're history, you dig?"

Ron hung up and sagged back into the kitchen. Francesca was sitting at the table in her overalls and T-shirt amid unpacked groceries. Ron noticed her flushed cheeks and how thin her neck and arms were. She had found a bowl and a spoon and had dug out the milk and cereal from the grocery bags. She looked up from eating her cereal. "I can't find Pickles. Is she outside?"

Ron sat down. "Francesca —"

"Frankie."

"Frankie. The Menace lied to you about sending Pickles to me. He never sent Pickles anywhere. Pickles was hit by a truck and died."

Frankie's eyes were huge and terrified. "Maybe he's lying again and Pickles is lost and scared." She slid off her chair and ran over to grab Ron's arm. "We've got to go find her."

Ron didn't think he'd ever felt so sad. "He saw her body, Frankie."

Frankie sank down to the floor and curled into a ball. She cried inconsolably. To Ron, it was the most heartbreaking sight in the world. Such a small child. Such gigantic pain. How could she contain it? Ron wanted a drink. Surely death and a heartbroken child were reason enough for a drink? He gathered up his sobbing little girl and gently laid her on the sofa, then pulled off his overcoat and tucked it around her. Then he went and got a bottle and a glass and pulled up a chair to watch over her, ward off ghosts. Protecting her, but mostly himself, with a bottle of gin.

Chapter Three

Ron Rudderless had good intentions. He wanted to be a good parent. But it was frightening and exhausting trying to figure out how to do it. He wished he'd managed to hold on to a few friendships so he could turn to someone for advice.

His first week with Frankie, Ron phoned in sick to work every day. "Terrible flu," he coughed to his supervisor. He couldn't face explaining why he'd suddenly acquired a daughter. The humiliation of letting people know that he'd once had a wife, that she'd left him for an electric guitar player named Menace, and that his own child had been sent to him on the bus like a crated puppy ... He just didn't want people inquiring that closely into his pathetic life.

He wasn't used to staying at home and soon wondered what people did if they didn't go to the pub.

Francesca had been such a little chatterbox when she'd first arrived, but from the minute she learned of Pickles' death and the treachery of Menace, she became somber and mouselike. That first weekend, she followed Ron around, watching his every move. He even woke up to see her staring at him, still wearing her hat, her intense eyes only inches from his nose.

"Gaa!" he yelped. Who knows how long she'd been standing beside the bed watching him lying there, snoring with his mouth open and face covered in red whiskers. "Oh ... Francesca ... awake already?"

"Frankie," she corrected.

"Are you hungry?"

"No."

She hardly ate anything. In the kitchen, he would bump into her and once he even tripped over her. It unnerved him. Ron had been trying to disappear for years and now he had a little shadow who never let him forget that he was very visible indeed.

"I've definitely got to get that TV fixed so she can look at something other than me," he thought, smiling uncertainly at her serious face as she watched him struggling with a dented saxophone. He'd started working on the broken instruments he'd been collecting for years and was slowly moving all the bits and pieces out of Frankie's room.

The only time Frankie was safely occupied was when she was gluing things into that scrapbook of hers. She slapped it shut whenever he came near. Not that Ron pried. He was terrified of offending her. The front said PRIVATE in big letters. She hid it somewhere in the junky room that was slowly turning into her bedroom. Ron might have been surprised to see her latest entry: a chocolate bar wrapper with the caption: "Sample of stuff from MY FATHER'S car. If I put in the rest of the garbage it would fill the whole book!"

Ron didn't go out to the pub for that first week of Francesca's arrival. It was extremely difficult. His nerves were shot.

"Are you sending me back to the Menace?" Frankie finally blurted at the end of the week.

"Do you want to go back?" Ron asked. The thought popped into his head that she might hate being here with him. Although he found the current situation about as comfortable as having his teeth pulled, Ron realized with a jolt that he didn't want Francesca to go away. She was nice. And she'd made him realize how empty his life had been before.

Francesca looked like she was about to cry. "Are you?"

"Am I? Sending you back? Well, well ... No. I thought you were going to live with me now."

Frankie flipped up the earflaps of her Peruvian hat and pulled her ears out from her head. This made her look like a brightly coloured bat. "Hmmm." She did a little twirl.

"Definitely happier," thought Ron, relieved.

"Well, if I'm staying here, I should go to school."

"School! Right! What a great idea!"

Satisfied, Frankie skipped into her bedroom. She got out her scrapbook, scissors and gluestick, and smoothed out the balled-up letter she'd found lying on the floor beside Ron's phone. After she glued it in place, she wrote:

Menace is a rottin lier. Good riddence to him!!!!!

The next morning, off went Ron and Frankie, hand in hand to the crowded schoolyard nearby, asking for the way to the office.

Ron forgot to give Frankie a housekey that first day, so she sat on the porch after school and waited for him to get home from work. Fortunately, it wasn't cold out. She looked drearily around: another house, another school, another neighbourhood. When she and her mom had lived with the Menace, they were always moving. They were in the last place the longest because Mommy was sick. Menace was away a lot. Mommy being sick made him nervous. You could tell by the way he kept jingling the change in his pocket. As soon as he got back from a road trip he'd start phoning for more work. He pretended other musicians were calling him, begging him to come and play, but really he was in the other room with the door closed, phoning and phoning. Frankie sat on the porch steps remembering. She wouldn't have noticed the stout woman in red running shoes going by except that the woman gave her a squinty look before turning into the house next door.

A few minutes later, a little dog with crazy eyebrows and little feathery fringes of fur around his ankles came trotting down the sidewalk. He was a terrier of some kind. He swaggered down the street bowlegged as a prizefighter, tail straight up in the air, obviously a dog of keen curiosity, observation and energy.

The dog was Dan Halberton-Ffrench; it said so on his

tag. He stopped abruptly at the end of the walk, overjoyed to see Frankie. He loved her at first sight. He decided to adopt her then and there and wagged his tail furiously to let her know. He would take care of her along with his beloved Augusta. He was a benevolent dog and allowed cigarette-scented Violet and awful cats and all those mice, skunks, raccoons, birds and bugs to live in the house. But they were his creatures and sometimes he gave them a good barking to let them know he was boss. Today he went marching right up to this small person and put both paws on her knees. He sniffed towards her face. She read his tag.

"Hello. It says here you are Dan Halberton-Ffffrench!" She leaned further down and *shlurp!* got a big wet lick on the nose.

"Gaak!" Frankie laughed. Nothing had made her laugh for a long time. Dan jumped down and got halfway down the front walk before turning around to look at her.

"What?" she called. "Want me to go with you?" He spun in a circle, which is dogtalk for "yes." Frankie shrugged and got up to follow him. Dan set off, confident and happy, looking up at her and grinning from time to time, happy to introduce her to his Daily Grand Tour: past the dingy houses, up the street, down the lane, sniffing the garbage behind the corner store, stopping in front of each house that had a dog living there and barking until the other dog was stirred to a frenzy. Then, very pleased with himself, he trotted off without giving the poor crazed animal a backward glance, peeing on every post and shrub. Finally, Dan dropped Frankie back at her house and disappeared behind the hedge of the house next door.

A week later, Augusta Halberton-Ffrench came to hear of Francesca.

"There's a scruffy child sitting on the stairs next door," Mrs. Slatternly reported, flapping a rag in the air, pretending to be dusting.

"Which 'next door' Violet? Try not to be mysterious."

"Him with the organ."

"There's a child on Mr. Rudderless' front steps? How long has he been sitting there?"

"A week."

"A child has been left sitting outside for a week and this is the first I hear of it? What is the world coming to? Violet! We must call the police. Bring the child in. Give him a blanket and something hot."

"Not left sitt —"

"Don't dither, bring him in at once!"

Violet Slatternly clomped down the stairs muttering about added workload and poked her head around the hedge.

"You! Little girl. Missus H says you're to come in for tea and stop sitting out there in the cold." Chilled, she pulled her sweater around her bosom. "Come on. I haven't got all day." As Frankie followed Violet through the opening in the hedge and up the walk, she peered up at the dark house curiously. When Violet had closed the front door behind them, Augusta shouted down, "Have you got him?"

"Yes, Missus H —"

"I'm a girl," Francesca piped up.

"What's that?" hollered Augusta.

"She's a girl," Violet shouted.

"Right. Well, take her into the kitchen. She can have an egg and beans, or whatever swill you're making for me today."

Frankie got fed in the long, narrow kitchen while Mrs. Slatternly prepared a tray for Augusta Halberton-Ffrench. Frankie was amazed at how impatient the old lady was. She was constantly ringing a little bell and shouting down commands. All the while, the stout lady in the black dress and the bright red running shoes muttered, "Yes, your highness. No, your ladyship. Whatever you say, Queenie." She turned to Frankie.

"I didn't always work in such a low-class neighbourhood, you know. My other clients were professionals with beautiful homes with built-in wall outlets for the vacuum cleaner. I didn't have to hump an ancient Hoover up and down the stairs like I do here. But I feel sorry for the old lady, so I keep coming." Violet picked up the tray and with a huge sigh started for the stairs. When she returned, she motioned to Francesca and said, "Come on. She wants a look at you. It's a good thing she can't see how dirty you are, is all I can say."

"It's a long way up," puffed Frankie, holding onto the railing as she climbed seemingly endless stairs.

Panting, they finally arrived at the top floor. Frankie stood in the doorway and gawked at who she saw sitting in an armchair by the fireplace. She was tiny, old and wrinkled. She sat leaning both hands on a knobby stick shaped like a "v" at the top. There were great big rings on every finger. Her chin and big bony nose were tilted up — haughty and aristocratic. Dark glasses covered her eyes and her gray hair curled into a stiff hairdo. She wore a blue blazer and blue jeans with a white blouse and a grey-and-blue paisley silk cravat. Her tiny feet were shod in soft, scuffed, brown leather.

"So. Now that you've been fed, you can tell me what your name is and where you belong," the old lady said in a bossy English voice.

"My name's Frankie and I live next door."

"Next door! Has Mr. Rudderless moved away?"

"No. He's my dad."

"I don't believe it! How can Mr. Rudderless have a child when he doesn't have a visible wife? ... Who's your mother ... Oh, good Lord!" Augusta leaned back with her hand on her chest and a look of sad astonishment on her face. "You're Cally's child."

"Yes, but she's ..." Frankie whispered the next word, "... dead. And so is Pickles. Run over by a truck."

"Your mother was run over by a truck!?"

"No, Pickles, my cat." Frankie swallowed a sob.

"Ah ... I'm very sorry to hear that." Augusta's voice softened. "Very sorry indeed — about your mother *and* your cat. A cat can be a true friend." Augusta took off her dark glasses and rubbed her eyes, then looked up unseeingly. Her eyes were milky blue. "God forgive us all," she whispered. Then she put her glasses back on and drew herself up. Her voice became bossy again. "And what do you mean, *Frankie*? Come now, what's your real name?"

"Francesca."

"Francesca. Ah well, that's encouraging. Your parents obviously had *some* ambitions for you. I was very close at one time to Francesca St. John Arbuthnot of the Devonshire Arbuthnots, who was the daughter of the great society photographer, Michelangelo Arbuthnot."

So began Frankie's friendship with the housebound, autocratic Augusta Halberton-Ffrench.

Chapter Four

"When I get up in the morning I turn on the radio really loud so Dad'll wake up. He has to get up now even if he has a headache because he's on his last warning at work. Then I do breakdancing in the kitchen to get warm. I'm a really good breakdancer. If the other kids at school saw me, they would be amazed." Frankie and Augusta had finished their tea and toast one afternoon after school. Now Frankie was sitting on Augusta's enormous bed sorting through the tangled glitter of Augusta's jewelry box.

"Whatever breakdancing is. The point is, do you ever manage to get any nourishment into you?" Augusta asked.

"I like to eat toast sprinkled with sugar and cinnamon. You have to butter it right away so the butter soaks in, and you have to have the sugar and cinnamon already stirred up in a bowl. Then you sprinkle lots on with a spoon. Then you tip the extra back into the bowl for the next time. I watch TV while I eat my toast and yell 'Dad! Get up!' in the commercials."

"Charming. And does he?"

"Does he? Oh, get up. I wait as long as I can but when the second buzzer goes, I have to run as fast as I can to school. I don't want to be really late. It is so weird to run across the schoolyard when it's completely empty and all the kids have gone in."

"Ah, blessed silence." Augusta sighed. They lived just down the block from the school.

"It seems as big as the universe, and the noises are so loud. I can hear my breathing in my ears and my feet are so loud on the stairs."

"That's because you can suddenly hear yourself instead of being drowned out by the screaming mob. Go on."

"The outside stairs to the school are concrete and make a concrete sound. The door has a wire cage over the windows. It's like prison. The door weighs a ton and I have to lean back with my whole body to pull it open. It practically pulls my arms out. Then I have to go all the way down a long wide hall to get to my room and my feet echo. When I get outside the door of my room I can hear the kids and my teacher's voice and I feel like I'm out in the empty universe. Inside is a warm bright one where they all know each other. I get so nervous thinking I'll always be outside, so I have to take big breaths to make myself open the door."

"Gad, what an imagination you have, child. Wouldn't it just be easier to go to school on time? Doesn't your father ever get up early enough to take you to school?"

"Sometimes. Then he makes coffee and his hands shake. He has Kleenex stuck to his chin."

Augusta snorted.

"He makes me instant apple cinnamon porridge," Frankie continued. "We can't face eggs in the morning. We only have eggs for supper with HP sauce and sausages and toaster waffles. And tea with milk and sugar. That's when we want to be healthy. Mostly we order out. When Dad gets up early he always says he's getting back in shape again and from now on everything is going to be different."

"Well, we know how long those intentions last," Augusta said sharply. "Mrs. Slatternly tells me you never comb your hair."

"Dad tries to comb my hair, but it is so ratty it just kills me and I scream so loud it makes his head hurt, then he trips over Germ and swears."

"Germ?"

"My new cat from the SPCA. But he's really Dad's cat. Dad gets annoyed because Germ loves him so much instead of me. But I think it's funny."

"Germ must be a particularly unsavoury cat to have a name like that."

"His real name is Jeremy, but when Dad comes home at night he says 'Go 'way Germ — Go 'way Germ.'" Frankie did a slurred impression of her father's voice. "Then he walks me to school and buys me candy on the way."

"Candy every day?" Silence. "Francesca? Anyone there?"

"It's not for me," Frankie protested. "It's for..." Her voice trailed off.

"Who is it for, if it's not for you?" Augusta insisted.

"It's for the bullies," whispered Frankie.

"Bullies! Who is bullying you? What did they do?"

"Oh, don't worry. They only got me once. They pushed me down and called me rat hair and said I stank. Now I give them candy at recess and they leave me alone."

"Have you told your father about this?" Augusta was outraged.

"Yeah. He sort of laughed and said it was good to have a sweetener for some people or they'll make your life a misery."

Augusta was disgusted. How could Ron Rudderless be so weak? "Well, report it to your teacher. This sort of thing has to be nipped in the bud or bullies will rule the world." ("They do already," she muttered, "but we can't just give up, can we?") Then pulling herself up, she said heartily, "I may be an old fool, but I know someone special when I see her. And you are, my girl. You are! There must have been a veritable mob of fairy godmothers gathered around your cradle when you were born."

"Real fairy godmothers?" Frankie was trying to lower yet another necklace over the tarnished tiara on her head. Bangles and bracelets slid and clinked on her arms. "What did they wear?"

"What did WHO wear?" Augusta asked.

"The fairy godmothers. Hmmm!" Frankie teased a cluster of diamonds out of the tangle and clipped it onto her earlobe. Her head pulled to one side with the weight of it and she set about looking for the second one.

"No, silly girl. 'Fairy godmothers 'round your cradle' means you were blessed with an abundance of natural gifts and talents. Didn't you ever read *Sleeping Beauty*?"

"No." Frankie clipped on the other earring and her head swayed like a flower on a slender stalk.

"No fairytales at bedtime?"

"No, me and Mommy read Jackie Collins."

"Oh never mind, you deprived creature. It's still true."

"I don't have any special gifts."

"Yes, you do. Come here."

"I *am* here."

"No, right here." Augusta smacked the spot beside her, raising a small cloud of dust from the decomposing coverlet. Snowdrop, another of Augusta's many cats, sneezed and woke up to glare at Augusta from one malevolent eye and meow a complaint.

"Oh you! Go away, you fat thing!" Augusta pushed him — plop! — off the bed.

Frankie stood up and picked her way across the bed. She sat down in the spot still warm from the evicted Snowdrop.

"Now!" announced Augusta, "for five minutes I want you to feel how I feel, to know how impossible it is to be blind." The old lady untied a silk scarf from her neck, and pulling Frankie forward, felt her face with cool, papery hands. She tied the smooth, heavy silk around Frankie's eyes, then slumped back exhausted against the pillows. "What do you see?' she asked.

"Nothing."

"Precisely! Nothing."

They sat in silence except for the thump thump of Frankie's heels against the side of the bed.

"Where's my walking stick?" Augusta asked suddenly.

"By the door."

"Well, go and get it for me, child. Don't dawdle."
Frankie reached up to pull off the blindfold but Augusta
put a hand on her arm and said, "Do it with the blindfold on."

Frankie slid down and started confidently for the
door, but as she stepped forward, her hand caught the
bedside table. Bottles of pills, drops and syrups clashed
together on their porcelain tray and a glass of water skipped
off and bounced on the carpet. Water arced through the
air and splashed on Frankie's legs. "Eek!"

"Leave it! Go on!" Augusta commanded.

Frankie turned and walked into a chair. Reaching
forward to steady it, she knocked it backwards instead,
entangling herself in the upturned legs. Her next step
came down on Dan the dog's paw. "Yipe!"

"Oh no, Dan, I'm sorry." Frankie reached down to pet
him but found only empty air as Dan wriggled backwards
and out of harm's way.

Cautiously now, Frankie held out her hands and
started forward with small, shuffling steps. Where had
the wall gone? How could it be so far away? Finally, she
was sure she had to be at the door and stepped boldly
forward ... and right into one of the unsteady towers of
books that Augusta collected. One stack hit the next and
books rained down onto a chest crowded with dusty
dried flowers, silver-framed photographs of long-dead
family and friends, and a mahogany tea box crammed
with old letters. It was a disaster movie and Frankie
was Godzilla. She reeled back and stumbled against the
curving leg of a spindly table. The table tipped and
Frankie tore off the blindfold to lunge helplessly for the

falling table as it went crashing to the ground, taking with it her favourite thing in the whole room — a lamp made of a small pewter elephant carrying the Earth on its back. She knelt down and picked it up.

"You've taken the blindfold off," Augusta accused her.

"How did you know?" Frankie looked up from tenderly trying to straighten the squashed shade on the lamp.

"I could feel it."

Frankie picked up the stick with the "v" at the top. It was a blackthorn thumbstick. The "v" shape was for resting your thumb when you gripped the stick. Augusta refused to use a white cane or make any other concession to her blindness. "Prince Philip uses one of these for walking on his estate," Augusta said. She identified with royalty.

"Everything's a mess, Augusta," Frankie sighed.

"Never mind, Mrs. Slatternly will be in tomorrow. It'll give her something to do instead of slurping down tea and wearing my ears off with her latest crisis. Now let's do it again."

"Again!"

When the scarf was back in place around Frankie's eyes, Augusta told her to fetch the small cloisonné vase on the mantelpiece that Frankie always admired because of the jewel-like colours of the enamel.

"Alright," said Augusta. "Before you go anywhere, tell me what's immediately in front of you."

Frankie pictured the cluttered room in her mind's eye. "Nothing."

"Wrong. Dan might be. Dan might be anywhere, or the cat, or a book or a bowl of porridge might have decided to sit there. When you're blind you never know what's been moved and you never know what no one's bothered to tell you. What's to the left?"

"The armchair."

"To the right — high and low?"

In her mind's eye, Frankie looked up to the small chandelier, then down to the floor where there was a thick, silk, turquoise-and-cream Chinese carpet with entwined fat roses. "The Chinese carpet."

"Exactly. Don't trip on it." And so on, until Francesca had mentally crossed the room and named each object along the mantel to the vase.

"Right then, now go get the vase."

This time Frankie crossed the room without incident by imagining the rug and the dressing table. Then she felt delicately along the mantel until she came to the vase.

"Aha," she breathed, curling her fingers around its fat little stomach. "I've got it!" she called.

"Wait! Feel with your other hand. Will you knock anything when you lift it off?" And sure enough, in front of the vase was a tall, twisted blue glass full of peacock feathers and a ceramic shepherdess with a lamb. They would most certainly have sailed off the mantel if she hadn't checked. Frankie tore off the blind and held up the vase triumphantly. "Ta da!"

"You see, a special gift," said Augusta. "You have powers of visualization and memory."

Frankie was impressed. She was wondering what her other special gifts were when Augusta said, "Now, come here. I've got something I want to tell you."

Chapter Five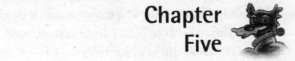

Frankie climbed onto the bed and perched, holding the precious elephant lamp.

"One of these days I need to find someone to take a journey for me," Augusta began. "I can't go myself. I'm too ill, too old and too blind. All I can do is sit here like an outraged cabbage. After that demonstration, I think you can understand why I feel that way." She paused, then went on. "I need to find something I lost a long, long time ago, something very precious.

"My mother died when I was a baby. I don't remember her. I wish I could, but I can't. When I was a little girl like you, we spent our summers in a house by a lake. Those were golden days. Children nowadays don't know what it's like to be free, to be able to ramble the fields on their own. All the gorgeous wildflowers, the songbirds, the jewel-like insects — they're all disappearing."

"Where are they going?" asked Frankie.

"The modern world is devouring them."

"Is that what you've lost?"

"We've all lost those things. What I've lost is a ring." Augusta held out her hands. They were long and bony and banded with rings — heavy hoops of gold and silver and encrusted with jewels. "No matter how many rings I bought, none could replace the one I lost.

"My father was a wonderful man. Clear-thinking, determined and brilliant. He always kept his promises and finished what he started. The thing that made him happiest in the world, he told us, was to be with his children. He used to carry me on his shoulders through the waving green fields, naming this flower and that tree.

"On my tenth birthday, he showed me my mother's cameo ring. It was a likeness of her face carved out of pink onyx and on either side was set a sapphire as blue as her eyes. That's what he told me. He said I could have it when my hand got big enough to wear it."

"What happened to it?"

"I'm getting to that. Father was a metallurgist. He experimented with something he called Human Responsive Metals which responded to the electrical charges created when we have feelings, desires and memories. He took a metal and polished and polished it with special vibrations by exposing it to a machine he called the Echofluctuator until the molecules in the metal were willing to align like small magnets to human contact. In other words, the metal *became like the human who was in contact with it*." Augusta stopped, "Are you getting this?"

"The metal gets person-shaped?" Frankie guessed.

"No, no, no. Here, I'll give you an example. You remember the ring my father was going to give me?"

"With your mother's face on it and the sapphires?"

"Yes, that one. Well, Father turned the Echofluctuator on it. Then Mother put it back on and the ring took on her personality and feelings. And how I know this is because my older sister Zelda told me that once when she was little, Mother had to go away. Zelda was crying and crying because she didn't want Mother to go, so Mother put the ring on a gold chain and let Zelda wear it until she returned. Zelda said it was overwhelming, she felt utterly surrounded by our mother's love, as if it had been magnified many times. It gave her an indescribably wonderful warm feeling of being held in her arms and her love. We realized that it was because the metal had aligned to my mother."

"Oh, I get it," Frankie said softly. It made her feel sad to think about being surrounded by a mother's love.

"I'll continue, shall I?" said Augusta. "My father worked with a Professor Proteus — we called him Uncle Curious. The two of them decided the metal would be excellent for a bicycle. They theorized that you wouldn't have to steer it because it would be aligned to your will and would just go where you commanded it to go. They made one, intending to offer it to the military for soldiers. In those days, bicycles were used for many purposes: there were military bikes, bikes for firefighters that had a hose attached, postal bikes, grocery delivery bikes and taxi bicycles. My father and Uncle Curious proposed a fleet of special self-steering military bicycles that soldiers could ride and shoot from at the same time. They wouldn't need to use their hands for steering, because the bicycles would just go where the soldiers willed them. They named the prototype 'the Hippogriff' after the creature in Greek mythology who had the body of a horse, the head and claws of an eagle and great feathered wings.

"But the bike didn't work like they hoped it would. The Hippogriff wouldn't go at all or went off in all kinds of unpredictable directions. Father was disappointed in the experiment, so he turned his attention to other things. He and Uncle Curious abandoned the project and dismantled the Echofluctuator to turn it into some other kind of machine. The only Hippogriff in existence was given to my sister Zelda.

"But Zelda and I discovered that the bicycle did in fact work, but in unexpected ways. It channelled intuition and magnified it like a microphone. We thought it was magic! Hippogriff seemed to be alive. We used to ride it with our eyes closed trying to produce a state of mind that would make the bike go where we wanted it to. It worked! And we also found that indecision and inner conflict jammed it and the bike simply wouldn't go. So you can see how the Hippogriff bike would be useless as a war machine. It responded to feelings, not commands or the will. It would be unreliable in war since so many young soldiers, once they discovered the horror of battle, would rather not be following orders but just go home to their families.

"In our games — I guess grownups would have called them experiments — we learned that the bike had a memory. Zelda would ride somewhere on her own, and when I got on the bike it would take me there and find its way back. The bike seemed to tune itself best to us children. So we realized from our experience with the bike that the ring was no ordinary heirloom, it actually was imbued with the feelings and character of our mother. We began to worry that the metal would realign itself to the next person who wore it. Would Mother be completely wiped out or would she linger faintly like a ghost? Zelda and I fought. We each wanted to be the first one to wear Mother's ring. I argued it should be me because Father promised the ring to me. This made Zelda very jealous. I was the youngest and Father's favourite. That wasn't fair of course, but I also believed it was rightfully mine because Zelda could at least remember Mother. Zelda had her all to herself until I was born. I couldn't remember Mother at all because she died so soon after I was born.

"You never lose the need for your mother's love if you lose her too soon," Augusta said wistfully. Francesca listened, feeling an ache inside. Augusta carried on, "Terrible things happened. Gruesome things. I can't even talk about them. Zelda and I fought and the ring was lost."

"What happened?" Frankie asked.

"My sister and I used to swim and row our little boat along the shore of the lake. One day, we'd been paddling and playing all afternoon when we heard a great deal of shouting. The dogs were barking and suddenly our two aunts came running down to the shore. They were crying as they splashed into the water to pull us out of our boat and carry us up to the house. Our father was dead. The next day Zelda and I were taken into the front parlour, where he was laid out in an open casket. Imagine our horror when we saw the aunts had placed our mother's ring on my father's baby finger. They were going to bury it along with him! It was as if they were going to bury our mother alive. I screamed and cried for them to take it off, that it had been promised to me. I pushed past them and tried to pull it off my father's big hand but the ring was stuck! I was picked up by my scandalized aunt, who called me a selfish little girl. I became hysterical and couldn't be comforted. They shut me in my room.

"The next day, my father was cremated. All the family and friends were there. There was a service on the lake shore and his ashes were scattered on the water from the end of the dock. All through the service Zelda's face was very white and the aunts looked furious. I seemed to be the only one crying for my poor father.

"Afterwards, there was a reception at the house and while the adults were talking and eating, Zelda pulled me outside and down to the lake. 'I have it!' she whispered. She held my arm so tightly, it hurt. I remember that her face frightened me. 'What?' I asked. 'Mommy's ring!' she replied. 'How did you get it! Let me see!' I cried."

At this point in her story, Augusta shuddered and put her handkerchief to her mouth. It took her a moment to continue. "Zelda got this crafty, smug look on her face. She said the ring was hers now, that she'd earned it. Then she took a little bundle from her pocket and was just starting to unwrap it when a hand appeared out of nowhere and snatched it away from Zelda. One of the aunts had followed us. This aunt unwrapped the bundle, and when she saw what was inside she screamed, 'I knew it was you! You wicked girl!' She took hold of Zelda and started to drag her away. I tried to follow them but my aunt whirled on me and cried in a terrible voice, 'You. Stay. Here.'

"I watched as she dragged Zelda down to the end of the dock. Zelda resisted all the way. My aunt's hair had fallen down around her face. She held out her hand to Zelda and shouted, 'Take it! Throw it in where it belongs.'

"I saw Zelda snatch the bundle from my aunt's hand, but she wouldn't throw it in. My aunt shook her. Then she slapped Zelda. I was shocked. No one in our house ever raised their voice, let alone hit someone. Still Zelda refused. 'Then I'll do it!' cried my aunt, and she clawed the bundle out of Zelda's hand and hurled it into the water. Zelda tried to leap in after it, but my aunt held on to her. I had no idea my gentle aunt was so strong, or could be so angry.

"I never got a chance to speak to Zelda after that. They sent her away. I grew up, and when the war started, I joined up and drove an ambulance overseas. After the war, time flew by. First you're a child and time is endless, then you blink and you're an old woman and you can't tell where it's all gone to. Along the way, life confuses you and you forget to do important things.

"But now, even though everything's changed, I know my ring is still there, in that lake. I can feel it. Feel it sing to me from the lake bottom. But unless I can find someone to go look for it, I'll have to give up hope of ever finding it again. And it has to be found quickly. It's almost too late for me."

"Why is it almost too late?" Frankie asked anxiously.

"I'm not going to live forever, you know," Augusta said briskly. "I want to have what's left of my mother before I die. Does that seem foolish to you?"

Not *foolish* exactly, thought Francesca. Maybe the word was *surprising*. It was surprising to imagine how someone as ancient as Augusta could miss her mother. Did this mean the sadness Frankie felt about her own mother would always be there? And then came a terrible thought. "Are you going to die, Augusta?"

Augusta laughed; but then she noticed that the animation that filled the room whenever Francesca was there was shrinking, growing cold and still. Frankie was pulling all her life energy inside, curling up like a hedgehog with the expectation of a cold winter that would never end.

"Francesca," Augusta said gently. "I'm very old and I *will* die eventually, but not yet. You and I will have many, many more conversations over pots of tea and many, many more of Mrs. Slatternly's horrible dinners. I'll let you know when I'm actually dying. You'll probably be jolly fed up with me by then and glad to be rid of me."

"Never!" exclaimed Frankie, horrified.

"I'm coming up with your supper," Mrs. Slatternly shouted from the bottom of the stairs.

"Francesca will be dining with me, Mrs. Slatternly."

"Oh, will she now, Queenie?" the housekeeper muttered to herself. Then she called up, "There's no chops left. I'll have to scramble an egg." She lumbered back to the kitchen, opened the fridge and glanced over her shoulder. She reached in, folded brown paper over the second chop, and put it in her bag. Then she took out the eggs.

Frankie was thoughtful while she and Augusta ate. She laughed minimally instead of succumbing to her usual hysterical giggles over Augusta's jokes in a cockney accent or recital of a funny poem called "Stanley and the Lion."

"Augusta," she said finally. "I could find the ring for you."

"Good Lord, are you still here? I haven't heard anything in so long I thought you'd gone home. Try not to be fantastical, Francesca. You're far too young to go on a trip by yourself."

"No, I'm not. I took the Greyhound bus here."

"So you did. But I don't approve of it and if I'd been consulted I would have said so. Someone should have accompanied you. Have I recited 'Miz Baker Was Bathing Her Baby One Night'?" Augusta tried to change the subject.

"Augusta, you said I had special gifts. Maybe I could hear the ring singing."

"I can see my best material is wasted on you," remarked Augusta. Then, with sudden fervour, she added, "Francesca, until you came into my life, things were bleak indeed for old Augusta. My little fox, with your pointed face and red hair, I can see you in my heart. I know you could find the ring because you *do* have special gifts. But not yet, little fox, not yet."

 # Chapter
Six

The next few months passed, spring came and went, and Frankie adjusted as well as could be expected at her new school. The teachers liked her, nobody *disliked* her, but there seemed to be some kind of invisible bubble around her that made other children's attempts at friendship just slide away — it was as if the glue to make friendship stick just wasn't there. Except for the little ones. She liked to help the little kindergarten kids and spent her recess in the kindergarten room helping. At first the teachers encouraged her to play outside with others her own age, but it soon became obvious that kindergarten was where she was comfortable, and besides, the little kids loved her. But there were still bullies. Just like in every school Frankie had ever been to, the mean kids came up in the schoolyard and pushed and taunted and threatened her. She'd been through it before. She didn't tell anyone. She just gave the bullies candy and they were a little less horrible.

At home, Ron Rudderless still had good intentions. He wanted to be a good parent, but it was exhausting trying to be cheerful and mature all the time, and it seemed to him that Frankie was quite good at taking care of herself. Plus, she spent her time after school next door. He kept meaning to go over and thank Mrs. whatshername, offer to reimburse her for any meals Frankie might have eaten.

"What IS her name?" Ron shook his muddled head. "Two words, H-something. Millions of rings. Mom used to be friendly with her. Yeah, and she gave me a little gold-and-silver band to give to Cally as a wedding ring because we had no money to buy one when we got married. Oh God, what a crummy neighbour I am." But Ron had left it so long to say thank you, he felt squirmy with embarrassment. Besides, the old lady scared him. She made him feel like a small, grubby boy who'd been caught stealing.

So even though Ron Rudderless loved Frankie more than he would have believed possible, the grey cloud descended upon him again. His head went back down and he started to disappear. Even from Frankie.

In Frankie's mind, her dad was either funny and kind with jokes and music, or he was The Zombie. More and more, it was The Zombie who came home after she'd gone to bed. Frankie always heard him come in because he fell up the stairs. He hardly ever walked her to school or bought groceries anymore. He emptied his pockets onto the bedside table, so she would tiptoe into his bedroom in the morning where he lay foul-smelling, whiskery and snoring. She gathered up change to pay for the candy bribes on the way to school and groceries at the corner store. He never noticed the money was gone.

But sometimes he was wonderful again. He would reel into the house early in the evening with a pizza, and a rosy cheerful face.

"Come on, Frankie Baby! Let's have a jam session!"

"Jam? Like jam and bread?" She followed him curiously as he dug through a clinking bucket of brass instrument parts until he found another valve cap for his euphonium, or rummaged for a slide for a tarnished trombone.

"No, jam, as in: Let's play MUSIC! Whatever pops into our heads. Just let 'er rip!" And he hoisted up the horn and played it while one foot beat the cymbal pedal and the other worked the bass drum. The cymbals clashed together and the furry mallet hit the drum *boom boom*.

He introduced Frankie to the penny whistle and showed her where to put her fingers to play little tunes called jigs. She started to carry the whistle in her back pocket and would sit by the window or in her bedroom by herself and make up tunes on it. In the jam sessions Ron gave her instruments to shake or hit, like tambourines or maracas from a trunk full of what he called percussion "toys."

"Isn't this a *real* tambourine?" asked Frankie, disappointed.

"Yeah, yeah, it's the real thing. Musicians just call all these little percussion instruments 'toys.'" There were sleigh bells for Christmas carols, shakers that looked like eggs, a cowbell, coconut halves for making the clip clop sound of horse's hooves in cowboy songs, ridged or rolly things, or things you twirled around, sticks and clackers, triangles, whistles, a small wood xylophone and a rainstick — an amazing hollow stick which made the sound of falling rain when you tilted it.

"Hit something, Frankie!" Ron roared. Or "Give us some rhythm," he'd shout, between blasts on the horn. Frankie leapt up and rummaged for an instrument in the toy trunk, then bashed away through another song. Ron always ended up on the organ to pound out some soul music with all kinds of crazy jazzy arpeggios. Frankie didn't know any of the songs but it was all great. She felt as if she and Ron were best friends, a team, fellow musicians.

When Frankie had first come to live with Ron, she was sure she didn't trust music or musicians. Musicians were mean or lied about your cat like the Menace. Or they were sad and drunk like Ron. Music seemed to make people unhappy. Songs made grownups cry and want to be alone. And just look at Ron's place! A musical instrument graveyard. Bits and pieces of dented, tarnished, cracked, unstrung, creaking, whistling, nonfunctional instruments. Sticking slides, vanished valves, cases with broken hinges and threadbare velvet linings and frayed corners. It was depressing. Everything was covered in dust and jumbled together. Sometimes she'd be woken up in the night by the sound of Ron rambling on and on, singing some sad song while he plucked an upright string bass or played mournful chords on the organ. Then he'd start crying. She felt like hitting him then. She hated the sound of his big baby blubbering and tried to block her ears and say "blah, blah, blah ..." to cut out the sad, infuriating sounds of her lost father. Then would come the crashes, curses and ouches as he made his way to the kitchen for another drink or finally stumbled upstairs to bed. The night felt so infinitely long and lonely when she was woken up like that. It made her stomach hurt, lying there desperately wishing he'd be the good Ron. If only Mommy hadn't gotten sick, or Menace been so awful. She'd blink back tears into the darkness long after Ron's racket had woken her up and he had finally fallen asleep.

But since the jam sessions, Frankie felt differently about music. "Come on, Dad. Let's jam," she'd urge Ron.

Sometimes he'd say, "What? Not now, Francesca. I'm not in the mood. It just reminds me of what a has-been I am." And Ron would avert his face from her bright eyes.

Or she'd say, "Teach me to play something, Dad."

"Not now, Frank. Dad's got a monster headache."

But other times, Ron would suddenly be in a wonderful mood. He showed Frankie how to make a big blatting noise on the trombone that was as tall as she was. He helped her push the slide up and down to make that roller-coaster sound. Then, just as quickly, he'd lose interest again. He never showed her stuff on the same instrument twice.

For Frankie's birthday in May, Ron came bursting in the door early with shopping bags full of party hats, balloons, a cake, a pizza and presents. He and Frankie sat at the turquoise kitchen table in the middle of the linoleum planets and stars eating pizza and drinking pop while Ron rummaged in the bags and presented her with all kinds of funny things: books, multicoloured flipflops, purple bubble bath and her own camera. It was fantastic.

"Hey Frankie! How do sailors get clean?"

"I don't know, how?" Frankie giggled.

"They throw themselves overboard, then wash up on the beach."

Frankie smirked but didn't laugh. Ron got a determined look in his eye. He took a bite of his pizza. "Hey Frankie! This reminds me of two cannibals I knew who were eating a clown."

"Oh, really?"

"Yeah, one turned to the other and said, 'This tastes funny.'"

Frankie tittered. Ron raised his glass of root beer and shouted, "Two slices of bread are getting married. Let's toast the happy couple!"

Frankie burst out laughing. Ron was laughing too, looking very pleased with himself in his paper party hat. Suddenly he slapped his forehead. "I almost forgot," he exclaimed, and raced out of the room. When he came back he was carrying a very small banjo with a purple ribbon around its neck. With a flourish he handed it to Frankie.

"Gee, a miniature banjo. It's ... old," Frankie said, a little disappointed. It was quite beat up with a faded ink drawing of Felix the Cat on the dirty drumskin.

"It is that," agreed Ron. "My mother, your grandmother, used to play it on stage before I was born. So now you can have it. It's a banjo ukulele — a banjolele. Everybody should know how to play something."

Frankie stared at the little instrument. Her grandmother! The thought made her heart beat faster. Ron gave her a little songbook with diagrams that showed where to put her fingers to make chords. Slashes below the words showed when to strum. She haltingly tried a few. But when Ron picked up the banjolele to demonstrate, the sound he made was wonderful. It was real music. It made you want to get up and dance when he sang, "Five foot two/ eyes of blue/ oh what those five feet can do/ Has anybody seen my gal?"

It was like that with any instrument Ron picked up.

"Oh Dad, you're fantastic!" admired Frankie.

"Nah, only good enough to impress little kids. Your dad just doesn't cut it."

"Yes, you do!" Frankie wasn't sure what "cutting it" meant, but when it came to music, she just knew he did.

"Don't you miss being in a great big band, Dad?"

"Nah, too much practising."

But somehow Frankie just knew that wasn't true. She and Ron had a birthday jam session. Frankie played the banjolele, going plunkety plunk when she strummed the four strings. Ron showed her three chords that worked for every song they played. It was amazing.

"Happy birthday to —!" Frankie sang. Ron stopped puffing on the mouthpiece long enough to sing, "You!"

Chapter Seven

A tinkling bell made Violet Slatternly look up from circling her favourite horses in the racing form over a cup of tea and a cigarette at the kitchen table. "I'm in the middle of polishing the banisters, Missus H," she hollered.

"Polishing the banisters! You'd do better to run the Hoover around."

"Done, Missus H."

"Done? I haven't heard it in months."

Violet took one last drag on her cigarette and angrily stubbed it out in a saucer, muttering to herself, "I'm too old to be climbing them stairs and you ringing and ringing your little bell like bloody Cleopatra on her barge." She scuffed to the foot of the stairs, and called up, "Ah well, you see, my brother put a silencer on it. The noise was shattering my nerves. I have a very delicate constitution. So he said, 'Let me fix that for you, Vi. Silence is golden,' he says. It's made eversomuch of a difference." Violet was slowly making her way up.

"Well, what about the washing up? The handle of this teacup is sticky. Are you rinsing properly? I told you to rinse with boiling water to disinfect."

Violet stood in the doorway of Augusta's bedroom. "I have indeed, Missus H. Everything is germless and uninfected. The house is inspeckible."

The phone shrilled. "Quickly! Hand me the telephone. I'm expecting the doctor. Augusta Halberton-Ffrench here ... Oh, it's you Mr. Drummond ... That's impossible. I sent a cheque to you three weeks ago. I suggest you check your records before you start accusing valued customers of nonpayment." She hung up and turned towards Violet. "Unbelievable! That was the butcher. Crookedest man I ever met. First he's pawning stewing meat off as steak. Now he wants to be paid twice. I know I signed a cheque for Mr. Drummond. I distinctly remember asking you to draw one up for $26.53. Did you spell his name correctly? Did you post it or deliver it by hand?"

"Post."

"I distinctly remember asking you to hand deliver it on your way home. Why *can't* you do as you are asked? And you *must* tell me or how am I to know what's going on? I cannot *abide* people going over my head or behind my back."

"It was my sciatica, missus. I didn't want to worry you with my health."

"Well, that's a first. It seems the only thing I ever hear

about is your health. And by the way, how is that sudden onset of neuralgia you were suffering from on Tuesday?"

Violet Slatternly's voice took on an injured tone. "Sarcasm! Missus H, you wrong me."

"Oh, I do apologize!"

The doorbell rang. "Quickly, Violet, that must be the doctor. Everything is ready for after?"

"Shipshape, Captain H."

"That'll be quite enough from you, Mrs. Slatternly."

The new Dr. Goldberg was young and efficient. He resented having to make a home visit. He preferred to see a waiting room full of people impatient to see him. It made him feel important. But his uncle, the old Dr. Goldberg, had assured him when he handed over his practice that it was just a few old people and they wouldn't last long, then he could run his practice as he liked. The new doctor put his foot down about weekends, however. After Friday afternoon, he was incommunicado.

The doctor put away his examining instruments. "Mrs. Halberton-Ffrench ... May I call you Augusta?"

"You may not."

The doctor pressed his lips together, annoyed. He became brutally frank. "You are completely blind in your right eye and the left eye has degenerated since I last saw you. I urge you to reconsider the surgery. There is a small risk, but only a very slight one, and in the end what difference does it make as you're going blind anyway?" Augusta winced, but the doctor didn't notice and carried on. "I'm sure the procedure will be entirely successful, which means it will radically improve the sight in your good eye. It's a very quick procedure. You'll be home from the hospital the same day if you wish. Your quality of life could be vastly improved. Wouldn't you like to see your grandchildren?"

"Since I've never had children, I don't see how I'm supposed to have grandchildren," Augusta snapped. She wished things didn't have to change, that one's old, friendly, caring doctor wasn't being replaced by a young, self-satisfied one. Then she sighed. "But there is one child I would like to see."

"Well then, what's the holdup? Look, Mrs. Halibut-Stench —"

"Halberton-Ffrench. Really, doctor!"

"What? Oh, I'm sorry. Look, I've had a cancellation. You could come in for the operation next Thursday. You're very lucky. Normally you'd have to wait months."

After the doctor left, Augusta mulled. She was getting old and there were a few things she wanted to set right before it was too late. And there was Francesca, who had become so important in her life.

Downstairs, Violet Slatternly hunched at the kitchen table, labouriously writing in Augusta's chequebook. She filled in the date and the amount and made the cheque payable to herself, Mrs. V. Slatternly. Then she hauled herself to her feet and up the stairs to Augusta's bedroom.

"What's this?"

"It's the cheque for the man who does the garden. It's real pretty right now with all the late spring flowers."

"Oh really? What's he got in there? I can't smell a thing."

Violet froze. "Ah well ... There's some lovely ..." Violet

thought of the pots she's seen in the supermarket. "Chrysanthemums."

"Chrysanthemums in May! That's astonishing."

"Well, maybe that's not what they're called. Pink thingies — you know?"

"Dianthus? Scented Stock?"

"That's it! Scented Stockings."

"Really! I'll have to go out for a closer sniff."

"Oh no, Missus H. One of the back steps is broken. You'll fall, for sure. Break your hip, get pneumonia and die horribly."

"Really, Violet, how vividly you portray my demise. Well, you'd better have that step seen to. Could you call Mr. Tashimoto? The elder, not the junior. The son's an idiot." Augusta signed the cheque, muttering, "More expenses. The house is falling down around my ears."

The doorbell rang. Violet jumped up guiltily, stuffing the cheque into her apron pocket. She headed downstairs for the door, complaining, "It's turning into Victoria Station in this house."

A few minutes later, Francesca and Dan bounded up the stairs.

"Augusta, look!" called Frankie. "I got a camera for my birthday. I can put your picture in my scrapbook."

"I never allow photographs. You may do a drawing."

"Oh," said Frankie, crestfallen.

"You'll find sketching things in the third desk drawer," Augusta continued.

Frankie put down her camera and fetched the drawing materials. Augusta's name was on the cover of the sketchbook. It was half full of drawings of landscapes and flowers. They were dated from thirty years before.

"This sure is an old sketchbook. How did you remember where to find it?"

"As long as everything is put back where it belongs, I can find everything." *Well, almost everything,* Augusta added silently, thinking of the ring.

Frankie was already concentrating on her drawing. She started with Augusta's dark glasses and carefully filled them in with solid black. Then she drew Augusta's large bony nose coming down from the bridge of the sunglasses. She made a straight smudge for the mouth with long lines going down from each corner. Then there was the silk cravat Augusta wore inside the neck of her tailored shirt. Finally she drew her grey hair which flipped up stiffly at the bottom and covered her ears.

"I'm glad I don't have to draw your ears," she remarked. "Ears are hard." She made a dotted line to show where the hairline swept back from Augusta's narrow lined forehead, then drew in a few more wrinkles. Augusta posed magnificently, as if she'd been sitting for artists' portraits all her life.

"There." Frankie put her pencil down.

"I can tell it's a good drawing," Augusta pronounced.

"It looks like you," Frankie agreed.

"Will you be pasting it into your scrapbook?"

"Definitely."

"Good. Tea?"

"Okay."

Augusta tinkled her little bell. Before long they heard Violet huffing up the stairs, but instead of her usual annoyed or martyred expression, she was smiling broadly. She started to sing, "Happy Birthday ..." as soon as she walked into the room. Augusta joined in. Violet put the tray down on a table and Frankie now noticed with pleased surprise that the table had been decorated with a pink cloth and a vase of carnations.

"Would you care to join us, Violet?" asked Augusta.

"Don't mind if I do, Missus H." She picked up the teapot. "Shall I be mother?"

Augusta giggled girlishly. "Oh do. And what have you got for us?"

"Well, hot scones with jam and cream —"

"Ooooh, jam!" Augusta cooed.

"Cucumber and cream cheese sandwiches with the crusts cut off —"

"Ooh, yum yum." Augusta tucked her napkin under her chin.

"Some lovely little cakes with pink icing rosettes."

"Ooooh, treats!" Augusta rubbed her ringed hands together. She looked about ten years old.

Violet turned to Francesca, "One lump or two, madam?" Violet held a sugar cube with a small pair of tongs over Frankie's teacup.

"Three, please." Frankie felt happiness spreading over her like sunshine as she watched Violet fill the rest of her teacup with milk.

Later, after Violet had cleared up and gone home, Frankie lay across the foot of Augusta's bed staring at the ceiling, eating chocolate-covered snowballs — her birthday present from Violet — and lazily watching the glittering crystal drops of the chandelier. She marvelled at the pretty rainbow lights they cast on the wall and ceiling. Augusta was sitting in her chair with her head back, glasses off and eyes closed, and Dan was conked out, lying on his side on the floor. They were listening to classical music.

"Augusta?"

"Hmm?"

"How did you know my drawing was good?"

"Because I could hear it."

Frankie turned over to lean on her elbow and stare at Augusta.

"I can hear paintings and drawings," Augusta continued. "They sing to me. If they're awful, they make a terrible screechy noise and I can't bear to have them in the room. Your drawing made a pretty little children's song. I knew I'd like it if I could see it. I can walk into any room and point to a thing of genuine beauty. It calls to me. Do you see all these paintings?"

Frankie looked around the amazing bedroom. Every inch of wall space was taken up with paintings.

"Art and books were my reason for being alive. I collected all these when I could still see, until my vision started to degenerate thirty years ago. I was a photographer, too. One day I'll show you my photographs. I still have some vision in my left eye. I can even see you. You're a dark shape with light radiating all around you, so I know you're there." She took a deep breath. "My doctor tells me that with an operation I could see you a lot better. So I've decided to get a bit of minor surgery on my good eye."

"You're going to the hospital?" Frankie sat up, alarmed.

"On Thursday. They're just going to replace the lens and I'll be home the next day. Oh dear! I wasn't going to mention this today but it seems to have come up anyway. It's nothing really." Augusta spoke lightly, with a carefree manner she didn't feel inside. She felt down the side of the chair for her purse. She pulled out three white envelopes with the denomination of the bills printed in giant black numerals on each: "5," "10," "20."

She held the envelopes one after the other up to her good eye, then took two bills from the twenties envelope. She held them out to Frankie. "Here. This is for emergencies."

Frankie hopped down and took the money.

"Now look in the middle drawer of the desk. You'll find a small red leather purse. There's a spare key to the house in there. You take that so you can let Dan out in the morning and feed the animals. Mrs. Slatternly isn't in until the afternoon. Ask your father if that would be alright, and if you can come and help me into the taxi at seven a.m. on Thursday. Mrs. Slatternly will book the taxi and get me packed on Wednesday."

"I wish Dad could drive you but he's lost his license."

"I suspected as much. Don't worry, a taxi will be fine."

Very early the following Thursday morning, Frankie let herself in through the front door of Augusta's house. Augusta was sitting in the kitchen in her coat with her purse over her shoulder. Her overnight bag was in the front hall by the door. "Ah, there's the early bird. Bless your cotton socks for helping your old friend."

They went out onto the front porch. "Lock the door, Francesca. Mrs. Slatternly will be in this afternoon. Make sure you feed the animals and let Dan out tomorrow morning."

The taxi arrived. Then came the hard part. Frankie had to walk slowly down the front steps with Augusta behind her, a hand holding onto each of Frankie's slim shoulders. Frankie noticed for the first time how uneven the steps were, how they sloped in all directions. Listening to August's shuffling feet she saw that the cracked and broken pavement of the front walk, pavement that she'd run over hundreds of times, was actually a series of dangerous surprises. Augusta mis-stepped into one of them and suddenly jolted sideways, nearly pulling both of them over. The taxi driver stood watching them, holding the car door open. He looked fidgety and impatient.

"You should have told the dispatcher you were handicapped. They would have sent you a handicap car. Some drivers don't like to take handicap. Too much responsibility. I'm just telling you this."

"Oh right," Augusta said through gritted teeth, but softly so that only Frankie could hear. "I would have waited a month for a handicap taxi."

"Who will take you out at the other end? My insurance doesn't cover this," the taxi driver said.

"The hospital is expecting me. The nurse will come out." They finally reached the car, and Augusta leaned forward, running her hands, fingers stretched out and fluttering, over the edges of the doorway, door, seat. She crawled in on her knees. Once she was turned around and settled, Frankie ran back for the overnight case. Frankie's chest was tight with anxiety for Augusta. She leaned in and kissed Augusta's withered cheek, surprised to find it so soft. Augusta reached for her arm. "Don't worry, little fox. I'm your grandmother now. I shan't leave you. Not yet."

That night, Frankie dreamed of flying, soaring high over the schoolyard. In her dream, flying was like swimming, requiring the same concentration. She swept her arms back in big powerful strokes to go forward and up. When she was up, she was suddenly frighteningly high, so high the world looked like a map. Trying to go lower, she swooped down uncontrollably, careering down through branches and telephone wires, nearly but not quite getting tangled up. Then she was struggling to rise just above the snapping jaws of angry monster dogs who only had two legs, who went forward by tilting side to side from one stiff leg to the other. They were very fast. She woke up very early, frightened but sure she now knew how to fly. The feeling was overwhelmingly vivid and real. She got dressed and ran out to the empty schoolyard. She ran up and down, up and down, arms out, willing herself aloft. Trying to fill her chest with that buoyant feeling. Making little jumps as she ran, sure each one would catch and up she'd go. But she was so earthbound. So leaden.

The dream and her failure to fly hung over Frankie like a dark cloud all that day at school. She felt weird and empty knowing Augusta wasn't at home. After school,

Frankie let herself into Augusta's house to take Dan for a walk.

"Is that you, little fox?" Augusta's normally vigorous voice was weak. Frankie bounded up the stairs smiling broadly, but stopped, horrified, in the doorway. Augusta lay back on three pillows with a huge pad of gauze and tape over her good left eye. A trickle of clear fluid ran out from under the bandage and down her cheek. Augusta was breathing hoarsely. She held a wadded ball of kleenex in hands that gripped like bird claws. She seemed to have shrunk.

"Augusta!" Frankie took the old lady's hand. It was sticky and hot. "You're all by yourself!"

"Mrs. Slatternly didn't think I'd be back until tomorrow. She's coming in the morning."

"But you're so sick! Why did they send you home?"

"They needed the bed. They said I could recuperate at home." Augusta gulped for air. "It's gone septic. I told them to give me antibiotics because I always go septic, but they said to wait and see. They said I could go to Emergency if I needed anything. Can't they see I'm old and blind?" she said, her voice breaking.

Frankie's stomach clenched into a painful knot. Augusta had the dreadful certainty of death about her. Like Mommy had in the end. She was shrinking like Mommy had, and just lying there smelling and sounding and looking and *acting* like a dying person. Frankie felt like crying but she just turned around and did what she'd done for Mommy.

She went to the bathroom, wet a facecloth with cool water and rung it out, then gently wiped Augusta's face around the bandage. She opened Augusta's clutching hands and wiped the hot stickiness away. She gave Augusta fresh tissue to hold. She looked at the bewildering collection of pill bottles on the bedside tray. "Do you want to take some pills, Augusta?" Augusta told her the names of the medications she was supposed to take. With Frankie's help, she took the pills and capsules with tiny sips of water, then lay back exhausted.

"Play me something on your penny whistle, Francesca. Something sweet and warm to chase away death." Frankie closed her eyes, calling up every ounce of prayerful love and healing to send out through the whistle.

"Ah," breathed Augusta. "So many gifts."

After a while Frankie went downstairs to make tea, remembering not to fill the cup too much. She heated up a can of soup and put some crackers on a plate, but Augusta had one spoonful and felt sick, gasping into the bowl, "Oh, how dreadful this must be for you, child."

"It's okay. It doesn't bother me. I helped Mom when she was sick." It was true, the yuckiness didn't bother her. But she was terrified for Augusta, who soon fell into a feverish sleep. Frankie took the opportunity to rush home and write a note for Ron: *Come rite away! Augusta is Sick!*

Hours passed. It was dark and very late. Augusta's room was dimly lit by one small lamp. Frankie sat beside the old lady, pressing her face with a cool cloth.

Augusta was talking incoherently. She opened her blind eye and stared at Frankie in terror. "Zelda! What are you doing here?" Then she shouted, "How could you? How could you cut off Father's finger? In his coffin! Dear God!" She grabbed Frankie's hand, pulling it and staring wildly. "The ring! Give it to me. It's mine. He promised it to me. You have the bike. The ring is mine." Then she screamed one long terrible scream that stabbed into Frankie's brain. Augusta sobbed, "It's gone ... gone ... gone." Her voice became tinier and tinier, until she just moaned and wept and rocked her head from side to side.

Frankie's heart was pounding in terror. Her hands shook.

Midnight came and went. Finally the front door opened and up the stairs came Ron. "It's been a while since I've been here," he puffed at the landing. He came through the bedroom door red-faced and huffing. "Am I ever out of shape ... Dear God! Augusta!" He took one look at the old lady and his terrified white-faced child then half-ran, half-fell back downstairs and called an ambulance.

Chapter Eight

When Mommy was sick, Frankie would crawl into bed with her and cuddle with a book. Eventually Frankie had to hold the book because Mommy's arms got too tired. And then Frankie did the reading out loud because she always was a good reader. They read Jackie Collins and Mommy listened with her eyes closed. Then Mommy went to the hospital and Frankie stayed with the family next door, and now she was here. At night, now, she dreamed of flying. She had to save Ron from the monster dogs. She tried to lift him up but he was too heavy. She woke up with the feeling of impending disaster. She wished more than anything that Ron would stop being The Zombie. She wished he would be a dad you could trust and rely on.

Augusta came back from the hospital after a week. She was no longer dying but she stayed in bed rather than getting up and getting dressed like she used to. And she was completely blind. The infection had destroyed her remaining vision.

Frankie came to visit after school as usual, patting Dan and listening to music.

"You saved my life, little fox. I would have died without you," said Augusta.

Frankie didn't know what to say to this. She didn't feel like a saver of lives. She felt frightened and worried. So instead she said, "You thought I was Zelda, and you screamed."

"Did I? I must have scared you half to death."

"Is Zelda still alive?"

"Alive and making money," Augusta said scornfully.

"Why don't you just get together and find the ring? You could share it."

"I want nothing to do with that monster."

"Why is she a monster? Do you know where she is? Could you phone her? I could write a letter for you." Frankie leaned on Dan and muttered into his fur, "I wish I had an older sister."

"I heard that! Well, don't. Especially bossy elder sisters named Zelda. Sisters are apt to come between you and your beloved father and spend all their time scrounging pennies and worshipping their bankbooks instead of things that matter, like art. They refuse to give you a loan to go to Paris to study photography. They try to make you go to secretarial school instead of following your heart's desire, which is to open an art gallery. Zelda was a greedy girl and she's a greedy adult. I do not recommend having a sister!"

"Oh, so you did see her again after you lost the ring?"

Augusta sighed. "Yes, I know where she is. She's there at the lake where we lost it. She bought the land around the lake and built a hotel on the shore."

"So why don't you call her? Maybe she's found the ring."

"I have. You don't understand. I haven't told you the whole story. It's terrible, gruesome."

Frankie sat bolt upright, all ears.

Augusta sighed. "That night when she took the ring, she tried to pull it off my dead father's finger. But the ring was deeply imbedded in the flesh. So she went and got a knife and *cut off our father's finger!*"

Frankie's skin prickled all over. She felt her mouth stretching down in a grimace of dismay.

"Years later, when I asked her about it, all she could say for herself was, 'Don't be stupid, it didn't hurt. He was dead. He wanted us to have it.' She still maintained she hadn't cut the ring off. What nonsense! The aunts certainly didn't believe Father's finger just came off by itself. They called Zelda unnatural and demented, and sent her very far away to a very strict boarding school. A prison for rich girls, more like. When she got out of there all she wanted to do was make money. She went to the London School of Economics and has been rolling in the stuff ever since. She wants me to sell her the bike so she can hand it over to a research company, so they can reproduce it and develop Human Responsive Metals. She thinks she can make a killing in industry with it. That's the only reason she wants the ring, too. She's searched and searched and searched but she can't find it.

"No, I can no longer talk to my sister, Zelda."

⌣·

One morning a few weeks after Augusta had returned from the hospital, Frankie was helping herself to Ron's bedside cash while Ron still slept. School had just ended for the year and she wanted to buy a popsicle and think about what she should do for the summer. Other kids seemed to go on vacations. Her hand froze over the coins. There was a letter lying beside them. It read: "THIRD AND FINAL NOTICE." Her heart sank.

The phone rang. Ron groaned, "I'm not home," and rolled over.

Frankie picked up the phone. "Rudderless residence," she said, imitating how Mrs. Slatternly answered the phone at Augusta's.

"May I speak to Mr. Rudderless, please."

"He's not here."

"Well then, may I speak to Mrs. Rudderless?"

"There is no Mrs. Rudderless."

"Little girl, may I speak to your mother, please?"

"My mother has passed on to the Great Soul Band in the Sky," Frankie quoted the Menace.

There was a pregnant silence at the other end. Then some crackling papers and the voice said, "You are the daughter of Ron Rudderless of 729 Larch Lane?"

"Yes."

"And you say your mother is deceased?"

"Quite diseased," answered Frankie solemnly.

Ron became dimly aware that his daughter was answering far too many, possibly incriminating, questions.

He hauled himself upright, quivering. He was wearing boxer shorts, one sock, and a shirt and tie. He took the phone from Frankie.

"Horg," he croaked. He tried again. "Hello? ... Yes, this is Ron Rudderless." The voice carried on for quite some time. Ron stood up. He sank down again and rested his forehead in his hand. Tears plopped onto his knees. He nodded from time to time, and finally croaked out, "Yes, I understand ... Yes, I'll be in to pick up my things tomorrow." He hung up, sagged back and pulled the covers over his head.

"Dad, aren't you going to work?"

A muffled "Bumpety bump bump" came from under the covers. Frankie punched him. "Dad, answer me."

"Not today."

"Tomorrow?"

"Bumpety bump bump."

Social worker Marisa Tomelle drove up Larch Lane looking for number 729. Months ago, a neighbour had phoned the local school to report that Francesca Rudderless was being bullied and the parent was neglectful. But the school didn't act on the information right away. Eventually a message had been passed onto the ministry, then there was more delay while a social worker was assigned. And then the file had sat on Marisa's desk while she hectically tried to catch up on her heavy caseload. Today was her first opportunity to look into the matter even though the file had been on her desk for nearly a month. She was feeling guilty and worried as she parked the car. She gathered up her leatherette briefcase and checked her face in the rearview mirror: tired eyes, frizzy hair and no lipstick. She sighed and dug through her pockets for a lipstick. It was pink and ridiculously cheerful for her worn but kindly face.

Frankie opened the door. Marisa looked down at the thin, pale child with yellowish skin. Her dull, tangled hair had bangs that tilted up from one eyebrow; it looked as if the child had cut her hair herself. She wore red rubber boots and pink shorts with a tattered T-shirt and a pearl necklace. Her knees, neck and ears were dirty.

"Is your father home?" asked Marisa kindly.

"He just stepped out," Frankie said, repeating what Ron had told her to say. He had said he was just running to the store for milk to put in the tea, but that was an hour ago. Frankie had a feeling he wasn't going to come back for their first meeting with Ms. Tomelle.

"Francesca, I'm Marisa Tomelle, your social worker."

"I'm Frankie." Frankie offered Ms. Tomelle her hand to shake. Marisa took it. It was sticky and grubby-feeling. The dirty fingernails had flaking red nail polish on them.

"I've come for a little visit with you and your father to see how the two of you are doing."

"Without a mother, you mean?"

"Not necessarily. Just to see if you are happy and well cared-for. May I come in?" Marisa asked, noting the violet smudges under the little girl's eyes. "How do you sleep, Francesca. I mean, Frankie?"

"Um. Okay, I guess. I worry about Dad. I can't sleep until he gets home."

Everywhere Marisa walked in the house, she saw

piles of junk, layers of dust and neglect. Marisa made a note. "So does anyone look in on you? Do you have a babysitter or a neighbour?"

"Oh yes," cried Frankie, eager to contribute something positive. She had a feeling the lady was not very happy about the situation. "Augusta, next door. I see her all the time."

"Is she home now? Can we go see her?" asked Marisa hopefully, jotting this down.

But what the social worker found was an old blind lady in a fantastically decaying house. The place hadn't been properly cleaned in years. The poor old woman was very much in need of care herself. Marisa made another note. She suddenly felt overwhelmed with weariness and pity. "I wonder if we might have a few minutes alone, Mrs. Halberton-Ffrench?" she asked Augusta.

"Of course." Augusta turned in Frankie's direction. "Francesca, be a love and go help Mrs. Slatternly get us all some tea."

"Francesca's school reported that she was being bullied and not receiving adequate care at home," Marisa explained to Augusta when Frankie had gone downstairs. "Mr. Rudderless was supposed to meet me this morning. I wish I had been able to talk to him but his absence is one more factor that leads me to conclude that Francesca will probably need to be put into care until her father is better able to shoulder his responsibilities."

"Oh no! This is all my fault," Augusta said slowly. She became distraught as she suddenly remembered the call she'd made to the school several months ago, shortly after she'd met Frankie.

"I really don't see how."

"I made the call. I was so upset about Francesca's father not doing anything about the bullies. Something had to be done!"

"You only did what any caring person should do," Marisa assured her. "I'm sorry she can't be cared for at home."

"But she can stay with me! Surely you can see she's fine. Not as clean as she might be, I'm told, but that's easily remedied," Augusta cried.

"I'm afraid, Mrs. Halberton-Ffrench, that won't be possible." Marisa didn't think she could explain further without insulting the old lady. "I really think it would be best if she were taken into care as soon as possible." She looked at her watch. "Oh dear. I have another appointment. I'd better be leaving now."

"Francesca," Augusta called. Frankie appeared at the door to her room. "Please see Miss Tomelle out." Augusta's voice was wooden.

At the front door, the social worker fumbled in her bag for her business card. On the back she wrote: *Please call me ASAP*. She gave it to Frankie, saying, "Please give this to your father. Goodbye, Francesca."

Her voice is kind but her eyes are sad, thought Frankie as she closed the door behind the social worker.

"Tea's ready!" called Mrs. Slatternly.

⌣·

Marisa was just getting into her car when Ron came running up the street with milk in one hand and cookies in the other. He shoved them under his arm to extend his hand. He shook the social worker's hand vigorously, trying to show energy and efficiency. "Ron Rudderless," he introduced himself. "So sorry not to be here when you arrived. Realized we didn't have milk for tea at the last minute. 'Tea for two and two for tea,'" he sang, doing a soft-shoe on the sidewalk and trying to show what a fun, nice guy he was.

"Maybe we should go inside, Ron. I was just over at your neighbour's house."

"Certainly. Yes, yes. You've met Augusta, poor old thing. Her corrective eye surgery went wrong. Old friend of my mother's," he called over his shoulder as he hurried up the steps, kicking flyers aside, simultaneously trying to make Marisa see how tidy *and* neighbourly he was.

Marisa looked at Ron's puffy face, red nose, and swimmy eyes and knew what his problem was despite his smiles and jokes and breathless fluttering around the kitchen trying to find two clean cups.

The truth was, Ron had *almost* not come back to face Marisa, but then he was seized again with sudden determination to be a Good Father. Now he stumbled over Germ and all of a sudden felt like crying. Too many things were going wrong at once. He sat down with the cups, praying to himself, "Please God, don't let her take Francesca. Don't let me screw up again. I swear I'll reform." He thought fleetingly about his last day at work, when he'd started up an impromptu jam session in his office with two street musicians. His bottle came out of the drawer and was passed around. Evidently, they were so loud the mayor himself came down to find out what was going on. He remembered calling his Worship "an uptight old poop." The old poop had fired him on the spot.

Ron suddenly became aware that the social worker was talking to him.

"Mr. Rudderless ... Ron. Has it occurred to you that your daughter Francesca is surrounded by adults who need her to look after them instead of the other way around?" Marisa leaned forward, staring at Ron.

He huffed, "That's ridiculous ..."

"Let me be frank. It is obvious to me that you have a drinking problem and your neighbour is an elderly woman of failing health. I understand that Francesca's mother recently died of cancer. This child needs a caring responsible grownup in her life."

Ron slumped. Defeat was his oldest companion. "You're right."

Marisa asked Ron a lot of questions, making notes and filling in forms. She pulled some written materials from her briefcase. "This is a referral for addictions counselling. And this pamphlet lists all the support groups available in the city. I strongly suggest you consider joining one. It will strengthen your case when you apply to have Francesca returned."

"Returned?"

Ms. Tomelle sighed. "Francesca doesn't have to stay in care long. Just until you get over this rough patch. You need to resolve your issues and find new employment. You need to provide a more healthy atmosphere," she looked around the room meaningfully, "for a child. Look, I'll give you another week. If you can show me a clean house, food in the cupboards, that you're enrolled in an addictions program and have some means of financial support, I will reassess."

Meanwhile, next door, Augusta and Frankie were drinking the tea Mrs. Slatternly had been asked to make before the social worker left so suddenly. Both were lost in their own thoughts.

"If only Dad had come home like he said he would. Everyone seemed upset about it," Frankie thought glumly.

Augusta, for her part, was making up her mind. It sounded like the social worker was going to take Francesca away immediately. It was her fault that things had come to this, and it was up to her, Augusta, to fix things. Emergency action was called for.

"I think," Augusta said slowly, putting her cup down, "that I will take you up on your offer to find my ring after all."

Chapter
Nine

Later that evening, Augusta stared up at a great starry sky only she could see. Frankie waited patiently.

Augusta contemplated. She frowned. She pulled on her ear. Then she clapped her hands together. "Hippogriff will take you to the lake and the ring, and Dan will point the way. The bike knows where to go because it holds my memories. Dan's memory will be an added reinforcement. You can't possibly go wrong with them."

"But Augusta. Where's the bicy —"

"Don't quibble." Augusta was in full flow and didn't want to be interrupted. "I hate people being tiresome about details. See if you can get your father on the phone for me."

Frankie spun the heavy dial of the old, curvy black phone, then handed the receiver over to Augusta. Augusta held it to her ear with both hands. She covered the mouthpiece and whispered to Frankie, "He's back."

"Ah! Mr. Rudderless. So glad to find you at home at last. Augusta Halberton-Ffrench here. You recognized my voice? How extraordinary! I had no idea I was so readily identifiable."

Ron listened helplessly, wincing under Augusta's irony. "Augusta, I'm so sorry I haven't phoned before. You've been so wonderful to Frankie. You're a great neighbour. I'm a lousy one."

Augusta dropped her formal tone. "Nonsense. You were there in my hour of need. I would have died if you hadn't called that ambulance. Now, I don't want to add to your troubles, but could you possibly let Francesca stay with me for a day or two? As you know, my old eyes have failed me and I need some help finding some papers for the lawyers."

"No, that would be a help, actually. I have quite a few things I need to do," Ron said, thinking of all the agencies he was going to have to see in the next few days if he was going to clean up his act enough to keep Frankie.

"Excellent. Don't despair, Ron. Everything's going to work out," said Augusta, thinking of her plan.

"I hope so," responded Ron, worrying about his.

Augusta handed Frankie the phone and rubbed her beringed hands together with the dry, scuffling sound of autumn leaves. "I shall be having a talk with you, Mr. Rudderless," she said to herself. Then brightly, "That's that taken care of."

"Augusta!" Frankie roared, unable to contain herself any longer.

"What?! Child, don't bellow."

"*Where's the bike?*"

Augusta looked surprised. "Here, of course!"

Frankie looked around.

"In the back shed," explained Augusta. "It's always been here. The key is hanging up by the back door. You'll have to put a drop or two of oil in the lock. The shed hasn't been opened in eons." Then, with the exultant air of a general planning a campaign, she ordered, "Right! We need brain food. Go downstairs and heat up some milk in the yellow saucepan. One level teaspoon of sugar in each cup and a sprinkle of cinnamon. I want the blue mug."

Frankie scampered out of the room and slid down the banister. Augusta lay back against her pillows with an expression of intense concentration and clasped her hands. What she needed to do was get Francesca out of the way for a few days to buy some time. Hippogriff would keep her safe.

Frankie skated on her socks down the hall, past dusty gilt frames and a naked bronze fairy on a pedestal, slim ankles poised and an inverted bluebell for a cap.

"And don't forget the chocolate Hobnobs!" Augusta's voice echoed down the hall.

Frankie pulled a green wooden footstool up to the old gas stove and stood on it to stir the milk with a wooden spoon. Blue flames flickered beneath the pot. Beyond the frayed and yellowing kitchen blind, dusk softened the outlines of the neglected garden. When the first bubbles burst against the rim of the chipped yellow pot, Frankie quickly turned off the gas. She used both hands to pour the milk into the mugs and fumed with frustration as milk slopped and pooled on the counter then dripped to the faded linoleum below.

"Francesca! Have you died down there?"

Frankie whistled as she tottered down the dim hallway with the tray. She laboured up the two narrow flights of stairs. As she puffed into the bedroom she remembered to ask, "What about Zelda? Won't she notice me when I arrive at the lake?"

"There's no reason why you'd even run into Zelda. She's the owner of the hotel there so she'll be in her office counting her money. She doesn't know you. It's a busy resort." Augusta had a sudden reservation, "You can swim, can't you? The ring shouldn't be too far out, but you wouldn't be afraid to hold your breath and dunk underwater, would you?"

"I have my Seal Swim Badge."

"Which means?"

"I can swim a width, tread water for fifteen seconds, do the flutter-kick on my back, jump in the deep end, and dive to the bottom of the shallow end for a rubber ring."

"That'll do."

"But Augusta," worried Frankie. "What am I going to tell Dad?"

"You leave that to me. Your father and I are going to have a long talk. You just stick to the white lie I told him on the phone. Now, back to the task at hand." Augusta was relishing getting ready for action. "You'll need a map. Dan will go with you, of course."

"Dan's been there?" Frankie looked at the scruffy terrier as he lay beside Augusta with his chin on his paws.

Chocolate crumbs and empty mugs littered the bed. Dan's eyebrows bounced up and down and his eyes moved back and forth following the conversation. At the mention of his name he sat up and made an impatient sound, as if he was eager to get going.

"Dan's great great great grandmother was there, so he knows all about it."

That line of reasoning sounded a little suspect to Frankie. "Augusta ..." she began, but Augusta was pressing on.

"Now, let me see. Two days to get there. Two days to get back. One or two days to find the ring. Let's say you'll be back in a week at the very most. That should give us plenty of time to clean up the mess here. You'd better set out tomorrow morning — early, I should think. Now, go to my desk drawer and get out the black leather address book. There should be a pen and paper there as well, and a map in the second drawer. I'll call my friend Mary. You can stay with her on the way there. Then you can stay with Professor Proteus on the way back. You'll be taking a circle route. Ready to write this down? It's been a while since I've been in touch ..."

Frankie looked doubtfully at the worn book. She opened it, and the spine fell apart in her hands. "How long has it been?" she asked, noting the faded writing on the yellowing pages. The map was in tatters.

"Oh, not too long. Thirty or forty years."

Frankie found and copied out Professor Proteus' address but couldn't find Mary's.

"Look up Dr. Dahliwal, Dr. Mary Dahliwal." Frankie found the name and wrote it down. Then she and Augusta went over her route on the map. Augusta remembered every village, town and stream, and Frankie was amazed, as always, at Augusta's incredible memory. Then she packed everything into her knapsack along with a small bag of dry dog food and a small plastic container to take the place of Dan's giant yellow water dish.

"I'll telephone Mary tomorrow," promised Augusta. "She's my oldest friend. We went to school together. She took care of the bike while I lived in England and has a very inquiring mind. She probably knows more about the Hippogriff than I do."

When Frankie went home to pack, her father was watching television. Germ was curled up in his lap. The coffee table was scattered with empty cans and the remains of a takeout meal. Ron looked up. "Come for your scrapbook?" He pulled some bills from his wallet and pressed them into her hand, and said to be nice to Mrs. Halberton-Ffrench.

"You can do that for Daddy, can't you, sweetie?" He looked at her with his sad, unsteady smile.

Frankie nodded. "I'm always nice to Augusta. Where did you go, Dad? The social worker came."

Ron looked away. "Unavoidably detained," he mumbled. He didn't want to burden Frankie with the threat of her being apprehended or the list of things he had to get straight in a week if he wanted to keep her. He waved at the containers of Chinese food on the low table, cold and half-eaten in the light of the television. Frankie took a foil carton of chow mein to her room, pulled off the paper wrapper and split apart the disposable chopsticks. She'd learned how to use them when she was little. She sat on her bed kicking her heels against the box spring as she ate, feeling excited and frightened about the next day.

"What are my special gifts?" she wondered and split open a stale fortune cookie. The slip of paper said, "Beware of ancient family feuds." She shivered. She didn't want to run into Zelda Halberton-Ffrench, that's for sure. She packed a bathing suit, a toothbrush, a sweatshirt, her penny whistle and her yellow-handled scissors for cutting stuff out to put in her scrapbook when she got back. She picked up her new camera, but then put it down. She already had way too much stuff with Dan's food and the map and her wallet, plus she was out of film.

On her way out she paused in the doorway of the living room, listening to her father snore. Then she crept up and leaned over the back of the chesterfield on tiptoe to kiss the top of his head. "Bye, Dad."

That night, Frankie slept in the sloping attic room at the top of Augusta's house.

"We'll say our goodbyes tonight," decided Augusta before bedtime. "I don't want to be unearthed at that ungodly hour." She held Frankie tightly for a moment. "God bless, little fox. I don't know what I'd do without you."

Dan sprawled on the landing, woofing gently in dog dreamland. Frankie tiptoed over him and up the narrow winding stairs, carrying the damaged elephant lamp to the room at the top. There, nestled in a cloudbank of pillows under a low slanted ceiling with Augusta's ancient one-eyed bear tucked under her arm, Frankie slowly turned the pages of an old photograph album. She rubbed her sleepy eyes as she looked at sepia pictures of two little girls in old-fashioned swimsuits and straw hats. They sat side by side in a child-sized rowboat, each holding an oar and squinting into the sun. The oars splashed into the sparkling water and the children seemed to be saying something. As she bent closer to listen, the sun set in the long-ago sky, stars twinkled one by one into the heavens, and a crescent moon rocked gently above the dark treetops. The little girls were now wearing fluffy nightgowns and ribbons in their hair, and the boat became a bed that sailed up from the lake and into the sky. She strained to hear, and sure enough, the sweet voices that rose from the page were singing a lullaby.

Frankie's eyes grew heavy. She sank back, lost among feather pillows, following the tune that ran like a road into her dreams:

Step over the sainted, snoring dog
And up the stairs to bed
Where a rectangle of blue
Holds a skating star,
And sheets glow coral
Under a small, squashed shade
That tilts the light
'cross Teddy's face
Where he lies in a heap at the head

Shadows on the slanted ceiling
Dance at your request
As night pours in and mother calls
Goodnight, my Darling,
God Bless.

Chapter Ten

"Bark! Bark! Bark!" Dan's furry face was right in front of Frankie's. He was standing on the bed, licking her nose, shoving his own cold nose into her ear and furiously wagging his tail as if to say, "Get up! It's time to get going!"

Frankie threw on her clothes, grabbed her pack, and ran down the stairs. In the kitchen she fed Dan and wolfed down some cereal. Then she tore out the door and down to the very end of the neglected garden. Dan galloped ahead, stopping suddenly in front of a sagging wooden shed. Frankie fished a large knobby key out of her pocket and, with the help of a small can of oil Augusta had told her she would need, turned the key in the rusted lock.

She pushed open the creaking door. Stashed behind a steamer trunk, cobwebbed with time, was a tall, old-fashioned bike with a swoopy black frame and a low, curved crossbar. Mounted on the cap in the middle of the handlebars was the equivalent of a car's hood ornament — a small winged creature, part eagle, part horse. Frankie wiped some of the dust away to read the flaking remains of curling gold script. It spelled "The Hippogriff."

She wheeled the bike out and leaned it against the shed, then lined its wicker carrier basket with a small plaid blanket. Dan was watching everything with bright, intelligent eyes. He sniffed at the bike and wagged his tail furiously. When he was picked up he knew exactly where he was going and leapt into the basket. Frankie grasped the handlebars and started to push the heavy bike down the path to the back gate. Hippogriff squeaked and groaned and the flat tires squelched flabbily. Gauze spiderwebs blew into Frankie's face. Her hands were grey with dust and dirt from the bike. Dan's weight made the bike hard to hold up and it keeled and leaned. She hit her shin on the jutting pedal as she jolted the bike into a big round stone at the edge of a defunct flowerbed. Dan went flying through the air with time for only the tiniest of surprised yips as the bike lurched from her hands. It fell to the ground with such a crash she just knew she'd wrecked it. Frankie sat down with a thump on the dew-wet grass and buried her face in her dirty hands.

Then Augusta's words of the night before came to her: "The Hippogriff is powerful. You just need to focus, little fox, and it will respond. All you need to say is 'Hippogriff, don't fail me now,' and it never will. Remember, my girl, I can spot someone special, and that you are. You are!"

Frankie sniffed back her tears, wiped her wet face with her palms, and said timidly, "Hippogriff, don't fail me now."

The bike just lay there.

She thumped her heels on the ground with exasperation and called out, "Hippogriff, don't fail me now!"

Nothing.

She stared at the Hippogriff angrily. "Some magic bike!" Groaning, she got up and started to go back in to tell Augusta it hadn't worked. Then she remembered: Human Responsive Metal. She had to *touch* the bike. She crawled over and put her hand on the frame, closing her eyes to concentrate. "Bike, don't fail me now."

Frankie opened her eyes. The bike looked less dusty somehow. Curious, she stood and began to heave up the frame, but found she could lift it with one hand. When she went to pick up Dan, the bike just stood shimmering all by itself, not leaning on anything. Dan jumped back into the basket. Frankie grabbed the handlebars and wheeled the bike forward. It felt light and smooth. Looking down, she saw with surprise that the tires were firm and full of air.

Out in the lane, Frankie stepped through the crook and put her foot on the pedal. She put her whole weight on it and the pedal sank down. The other pedal rose up to meet her other foot and the bike slowly rolled forward. She pedalled again and got herself perched on the comfortable old leather saddle. She pedalled again. It seemed as if the bike gained confidence with every turn of the wheels, swelling with motion like the sails of a sleek old sailboat.

Before too long they came to a busy street. It was frantic with traffic. A big truck hurtled past, sucking the air with a giant *Whump!* Cars drove so fast and so close to the curb, there was no room for even a bicycle. Frankie was afraid of the traffic but knew she had to go on. She pushed down on the pedal — it wouldn't budge. Stuck already! Dan turned and barked in her face. *Go Back! Go Back!* he seemed to be saying.

"We can't, Dan. We have to go find Augusta's ring."

Dan leapt out of the basket and ran back up the lane, where he stood hopping on all fours with impatience and running in circles. He seemed to be leading her back home again. "I guess Augusta forgot about traffic," Frankie thought. Wearily, she pushed the bike back up the lane. Then, beyond the waving perfumed lilac and overgrown clumps of grass, she saw a turn onto another paved lane that ran for miles behind the houses of the busy street.

"Dan, you smarty! That's much better for us!" Back into the basket went Dan, and the bike took off like a shot as soon as her foot touched the pedal.

Dan sat up with his paws on the rim of the basket, stuck his nose into the wind, and with great joy, sharply barked. "Make way! We're coming! Make way!"

And away they rode.

After a while, the houses became smaller and meaner. Garbage drifted and gathered in the corners and creases of the lane. Unpainted fences leaned, and old wrecks of cars and rusting washing machines took root in the rampage of weeds in forgotten backyards. They rode on until there were no gardens at all. Then the houses were replaced by brick buildings zigzagged by blackened fire escapes. There were signs that said "No Parking, No Trespassing, Keep out!" and stinking overfilled dumpsters.

Eventually, they rode around a bend to find that the lane led straight into a street market. Crammed on both sides of the narrow street were fruit and vegetable stalls, and stands selling just about anything you could imagine. Hawkers shouted the unparalleled virtues of their hats or video cassettes or hot baked potatoes or miracle tomato slicers. In a patch of empty road between two stalls, onlookers gathered to watch an old man dance around his upturned hat. He grinned as he sang, *"Pack up all my cares and woe/Here I go singing low/ Bye bye blackbird ..."*

Frankie got down to walk the bike so she could squeeze through the crowd. She walked past mothers buying broccoli while their babies gummed a bit of banana or leaned down from their strollers waving sticky starfish hands; past old people pushing shopping cart walkers; and around a group of gossips who formed human blots in the flow of people.

Dan ran ahead. Only his pointed tail was visible between the legs and wheels of shoppers and buggies until he disappeared altogether.

"Dan!" Frankie shouted, bobbing her head back and forth, trying to see him between the people. She hurried forward.

"Ow! Watch it, kid!"

"Sorry, sorry." Anxiously weaving her bike in and out, she didn't notice a hand unzipping and reaching into her backpack. But the bike did, and it reared and bucked

91

like a kicking mule. A voice behind her cursed. Frankie whipped around to find her wallet falling out of her pack. "I've forgotten to zip it up," thought Frankie, unaware of the would-be thief slinking back into the crowd. "I'm going to have to be more careful now that I'm on the road."

"Bark, bark!" Dan was back and looking pleased with himself. Then he took off again, his jaunty tail weaving in and out of the crowd. When Frankie finally caught up with him, he was sniffing around a junk stall.

The man at the stall had grey hair that stuck out uncombed from under his flat hat. He smoked a squashed cigarette and scratched the stubble on his chin with grimy fingernails. When he opened his mouth to speak, Frankie could see that his lower teeth were stained brown. He coughed, and peering down at her, wheedled in a cracked voice, "Something lovely for madam today?"

Mesmerized, Frankie watched as he swept his hand across a dusty velvet tray of trinkets and costume jewelry.

"Feast your eyes on this finery." His purple bulbous nose and creased cheeks spread as he gave her his most winsome smile.

Like a magpie, Frankie found it hard to resist the sparkling colours. Without meaning to, she found herself fingering through the tangle. Then something on the far side of the tray caught her eye. A ring just like the one Augusta had described! She held her breath; it couldn't be!

The man was watching her closely. Frankie reached for the ring but he was faster.

"This magnificent ring, for instance," he crowed, thrusting the tarnished old cameo under her startled nose. Two blue rhinestones flanked a scuffed pink profile. He tapped the plastic face with a cracked fingernail. "Listen to that. Genuine onyx. It reminds me of my dear muvver, bless 'er." He took Frankie's hand in his rough, nicotine-stained paw and slid the ring on her finger.

The ring was huge and just hung there. Now that she could see it up close, Frankie realized it was obviously not Augusta's. She could see the glue holding rhinestones, not sapphires like in Augusta's ring, and a tiny strip of shiny plastic coating had peeled back from the edge of the cameo. But still, from a distance, the resemblance to the ring Augusta had described was uncanny. This version might be useful to have. Frankie didn't know why, but it didn't seem right not to buy it.

"Do you mind if I show it to my dog?"

"Show it to your dog? Sure, sure, whatever turns your crank." The man drummed his fingers and whistled. He shrugged at the next stallholder. "She wants to show it to her dog."

Frankie crouched down and held the ring in front of Dan. "What do you think, Dan? Should I buy it?" Dan barked enthusiastically and wagged his tail. She stood up. "We think it's nice. How much does it cost?"

"Nice?! Madam, it's you!" the man roared. "Normally I'd ask a lot more, but for a you, a special price of $20. But that's my rock bottom price."

"I don't think I can pay $20," Frankie said, looking through her pack. She got out her wallet, not sure how much was in it, but sensing it would be wise to leave Augusta's envelope at the bottom of the pack and the money her father had given her safe in her pocket. She undid the clasp to reveal a much-creased and folded five-dollar bill, a looney and three dimes.

The man swept the money into his dirty, calloused hand with surprisingly nimble fingers. "I'll take it! Mind you, it's a sacrifice. I'm too soft-hearted, me. Always have been," he panted, unfolding the bill greedily and stuffing it into the wad he pulled out of the pocket of his stained corduroy trousers. "Here, let me fix you up." And he pulled out a length of hairy green string, threaded it through the ring, tied a knot, and slipped it over Frankie's head. "May it bring you luck. Now move along. You're getting in the way of my other customers with that mutt and that pile of rust."

Chapter Eleven

The Bike refused to go down busy streets but was fast and easy to ride down lanes, backroads and pebble paths along railway tracks. It would only take Frankie in one general direction. Eventually, she realized Hippogriff was leading her out of the city. She was gradually able to sense, by a gentle pulling of the handlebars and resistance in the pedals, where the bike wanted her to go, so she was able to avoid any more abrupt halts or having to get off to push the bike back to the last crossroads. She realized that Dan was helping her, and not just barking at cats. The bike was so effortless to ride she hardly got tired. And as she rode she started to feel extraordinarily happy, happier than she'd ever felt before with a careless, free exuberance. And going down hills! What an experience. It was like flying. Soaring with the wind against her skin and through her hair.

Eventually, Frankie and Dan found themselves on a narrow country road. The old pavement crumbled at the edges and sloped down to grassy ditches and fields. Not since her Greyhound bus trip had Frankie been out of the city and she looked around with curious enjoyment. "Going by bike is the perfect way to travel, Dan. You can smell the air, feel the sun and things go by just at the right speed."

The occasional car passed. People noticed the little girl on the high, spindly antique bike with a dog grinning over the fluttering plaid blanket.

"How quaint," they'd remark. "There goes the child of an eccentric country family." Or if it was a farmer in his pickup truck, he'd wave at Frankie and mutter to himself, glancing in the rearview mirror, "City people are so crazy about old junk. Why don't her parents give that little red-haired girl a nice new mountain bike to ride when they're visiting the country?"

It was noon when Frankie came to a highway. Just at the juncture where the old road met the highway, there was an old station wagon parked on the shoulder of the road. Handpainted signs said "Bumble Honey For Sale." A woman in jeans and a pink straw hat sat on the tailgate with her two blonde children.

"Try some honey, Honey," the woman smiled. Frankie slowed down on the crunchy gravel. She was hot, thirsty and hungry. She pushed her hair off her sticky forehead and watched the woman cut a thick piece of white bread and spread butter and honey to the edge of the golden crust.

"You look hot, sweetie. Wanna glass of milk, too?"

"Yes, please." Dan leapt down as Frankie laid the bike in the long dusty grass of the field. Grasshoppers sprang up with every step she took. The bread was soft and fresh. White honey bulged at the edge of the crust and tasted wild, sweet and flowery with the soft, salty butter.

"Good, huh?" said Mrs. Bumble. "Cheap too. Tell your friends, tell your mum, write the Prime Minister — Bumble Honey is beeeautiful."

Frankie sat on the grass in the shade of the station wagon and watched the two tiny Bumbles playing dolls. Dan the Dog and the Bumble Golden Retriever sniffed at each other, then ran off tumbling and circling. Happily exhausted, they slurped at a plastic bucket of water and lolled with tongues showing pinkly in panting doggy smiles.

"I think you need one more," said Mrs. Bumble, handing Frankie another slice and filling up her glass from the cooler.

Pails of honey disappeared as one vehicle after another pulled over. Frankie watched the children while Mrs. Bumble made change and emptied her station wagon of one-, two-, and five-kilo pails. Some people sampled a slice of bread and honey. Others said they already knew how good Bumble honey was and had waited all year to buy some. Frankie tried to help lift pails of honey out of the station wagon.

"No, no, no," Mrs. Bumble rushed over. "Not like that. You'll hurt your back. Lift with your legs. Your legs are the strongest part of your body."

"My legs?" Frankie imagined sticking a foot through the pail handle to lift it.

"Here, I'll show you. Keep your back straight. Bend your knees. Then lift by straightening and feeling the weight in your legs."

Soon all the honey was gone.

"Look at that!" exclaimed Mrs. Bumble. "We've just about sold out. I've got one little sample jar left. You've brought me luck and you've got a real gift with children too, Frankie. You must have little brothers and sisters."

"I don't. I just like being with little kids. I always thought that meant I was immature."

"Not immature at all. Just the opposite. Where do you live, Frankie? We can drive you home."

Before Frankie could think of what to say, an army of cyclists wheeled up, followed by a van marked "Wilderness Bicycle Tours." The hotshots sped off ahead, followed by average riders, and trailed by a wobbly mob of slowpokes, mostly older people and kids trundling behind.

"I'm with them," Frankie said, grabbing Dan and pulling up Hippogriff.

"Oh, well. Here, take this," called Mrs. Bumble, running over to put the sample jar of honey beside Dan in the basket. "And here's an extra label to keep. It's got our address on it. You come visit us." She put her arm around Frankie's shoulder and gave her a squeeze. "You're good company, young Frankie. Be sure to come and see us." Frankie looked at Mrs. Bumble's pleasant, tanned face and the crinkles around her smiling eyes, feeling surprised and happy that she'd made a friend.

"Bye bye," squeaked the little Bumbles, hopping and waving at the side of the road.

"Bye bye," Frankie called back as she hurried to catch up with the cycle tour.

Chapter
Twelve

Ron spent the day tromping wearily from one office to the next. He cleared out his desk and got his record of employment papers. Then he signed on for unemployment, went for counselling for his drinking, found a therapist for his depression and feelings of failure and inadequacy, and went to Social Services for emergency financial help until his unemployment payments kicked in, which would be a long long time because he'd been fired. At Social Services he was told he'd have to sign up for a seminar on re-entering the work-force. So he did that. After all that he was so exhausted he wanted nothing more than a few revitalizing drinks. But instead he went to a funky little café.

He sat in a booth and soon his attention was drawn to a jukebox directory mounted on the wall. It was encased in glass. Each page of songs had a small metal tag that stuck out the top so you could flip through and choose your song. He put a quarter in the slot and punched in H9 for "Who put the bop in the bop shebop shebop?" That was fun. Rubbing his hands together and smiling, he looked around.

"There's more light in a restaurant than in a bar," he remarked to the waitress. He followed his dinner with a large piece of hot apple pie à la mode. That was so good he decided he'd like a second dessert and ordered chocolate pudding with whipped cream. After that he felt almost as good as if he'd been to a bar, but he worried how his stomach would look if he had two desserts every time he felt like having a drink. Ron sighed to himself. "I'll just have to worry about my girlish figure later. The important thing is to keep Frankie." Ron reached under the booth where he'd stowed his briefcase full of the contents of his desk at work. He found what he was looking for — a framed birthday photo of him and Frankie in their party hats. To make it look like they were sitting side by side, Frankie had glued together the pictures that they'd taken of each other. It was goofy but nice. He felt tears start as he thought about the impulse behind Frankie's picture of the two of them together on her birthday.

She was such a funny, nice little kid. Taking care of old Mrs. H. like that. Probably Cally too, he realized sadly. And she was a good little flute player, now that he thought of it. Amazing, lovely tunes coming out of her bedroom when she thought no one was listening. She deserved something better than good intentions.

"You deserve a real dad," he said to the photo. Leaving

the photo and his coat in the booth, he took his briefcase into the washroom. He opened it on the floor and took out his bottle of gin from the office. He looked at it sorrowfully.

"Goodbye old friend — and enemy." With a look of determination, he poured the contents down the sink. Then, holding the bottle to his chest, he sang a funeral hymn in his deepest baritone:

"Ashes to ashes
The priest and the monk
From this day forward
I'll never get drunk."

"I consign you to the deep," he said, and he dropped the bottle into the trash bin. His voice echoed solemnly. Whistling "Onward Christian Soldiers" under his breath, Ron marched briskly back to his booth. He opened the directory of support groups that one of the counsellors had given him that morning.

"Aha!" He circled a meeting that started at nine o'clock that very evening.

He looked at his watch. It was only 6:30. Enough time to go home first. He decided to walk home and chose a route through the residential streets, enjoying the scented air and looking at the gardens and the houses. He was fantasizing about painting his house and restoring his mother's overgrown garden when he heard it. Only faintly, but unmistakably: a band ... a concert band, with all its lovely horns. He stood still, listening and picking out the instrument sections: trumpets, french horns, trombones, tuba, but no euph. He recognized the tune. It was "Carnival of Venice." He remembered that the piece had a killer euphonium solo which he had once practised until his lips and fingers fell off. Well, almost, but he'd gotten it right. Yes indeedy.

"Ack! You're ruining it!" he exclaimed suddenly as a new instrument started up. A trombone was butchering *his* solo! Without realizing he was doing it, he followed the sound. It led him to a high school. The gym door was open. Ears aquiver, he found himself walking in and down a locker-lined hallway now echoing and booming with music coming from a room — probably the band room — at the end.

The music stopped and an enraged voice called out, "Trombone! Why aren't you playing?"

"I'm lost," whimpered the struggling trombonist.

"Don't tell me about your religious problems. Just play the music!"

Ron stuck his head in the doorway. The room was full of musicians of all ages. "Must be a community band," he thought. The director turned and saw him.

"I don't suppose you play the euphonium?"

"I do, actually."

"Hallelujah! Get in here! Get the man a horn."

"It's been a long time since I played this piece. I can't stay for long," Ron stuttered apologetically as he made his way to the back of the room, his arms full of music, horn and briefcase.

In the break he chatted with the director. The man's name was Frank and he was an ex-rocker turned musical director for various community bands. He and Ron found they knew some of the same people from the music business. And before he knew it, Ron had agreed to act as a substitute for the director the following week because Frank's wife was about to have a baby.

Ron hurried off to his support group in a state of astonished excitement. He whistled "The Carnival of Venice" as he walked. Maybe everything would work out after all.

Chapter Thirteen

Frankie caught up with the cyclists and merged with the kiddie and older people pack. Everyone smiled and pointed at Dan riding in the basket.

"*Ciao.*"

"*Morgen.*"

"*Guten Tag.*"

"*Buon giorno.*"

"Hi, hi, hi, hi," Frankie replied to everyone who greeted her. It seemed that nobody spoke more than a few words of English. She rode and rode. Her shadow got longer and longer on the road in front of her and her stomach rumbled.

The group passed a roadside gas station and general store. "I wonder if we should stop and get some food at that store, Dan?" she whispered. But she was reluctant to lose this friendly group. And so far, Hippogriff seemed to like the direction the holiday cyclists were taking. They rode on, leaving the farmland behind. The trees got taller and closer to the road. The air smelled cool and piney. They came to a park entrance and the uniformed girl in the booth just waved them through. Frankie followed the group off the road and down a gravel turn that opened into a meadow. The van was already there. A buffet was set up and a barbecue was sizzling beside it. An awning that projected from the open side doors of the van read "Wilderness Bicycle Tours" in big bold letters. Frankie hesitated for about ten seconds, then laid down Hippogriff on the grass and ran over to the buffet table with everyone else.

One of the guides looked up from flipping burgers. "Look at that kid with the dog." He poked the spandex-clad woman working next to him. "Didn't you say 'No dogs'?"

"No." The woman's voice was defensive. "Why should I? Who brings a dog on a bike tour?"

"Well, it's too late now. You'd better put it into the brochure for next time. There are a zillion kids here and nobody speaks English. Look! No one's wearing their nametags. We're going to have to slap this group into shape or it's going to be chaos."

"Yeah, well whose idea was it to put a German group with an Italian group?" retorted the woman.

Frankie loaded up her plate and grabbed a pop. Looking both ways she shoved muffins and fruit and boxes of juice into her pack. A lady stared at her. "I'm going through a growth spurt," she announced, then giggled, "I'll probably be six feet tall by grade seven." The lady shrugged and walked away. Frankie wasn't sure if anyone understood her, so she just smiled at everyone, letting the Italians think she was German and the Germans think she was Italian. A pick-up soccer game was in progress and two groups of onlookers were singing their national anthems, trying to drown each other out. In the other direction, two men were waving wilderness manuals and yelling in English at each other.

Suddenly a bell clanged and everyone looked up. The tour guides were helmeted and gloved again. "Okay everyone, let's go," said the woman in spandex. "We have a ways to go before we make camp for the night."

⌐•

As the sun set, Frankie let the holiday cyclists pull further and further ahead until they disappeared over the horizon, leaving only the banded sky. Violet and magenta graded down to a lingering yellow, and high above, surprisingly pale blue swept away to the stratosphere. Here and there diamond-chip stars pinged into the deepening blue. It was almost night and there was nowhere to sleep. No safe corner to huddle, no hot bath, no warm drink. Frankie felt very small in the vast outdoors with only the road disappearing over the edge of the turning planet. Another star popped into the deep transparent blue ocean of space, and the moon smiled down a little sadly. Hippogriff refused to go any further.

"Hippogriff, don't fail me now," Frankie urged wearily, her lip trembling a little, but the bike wouldn't go and so she stood down on the still-warm pavement in the cooling night air. The road was smooth and black as if it had been recently paved, and the white stripe disappearing into the distance gleamed in the dusk. Dan took off, nose to the ground and tail high through the whispering, cricketty grass. Sighing, she found the bike would go only when she turned off the road and followed him. She bumped down through a shallow ditch and up the bank through rough, dry grass and scratchy wildflowers with a musky, sagey perfume. At the top of the bank, she turned and saw the land stretching for miles and the last glow of topaz at the horizon as the sun sighed and sank beneath the cover of distant foothills.

Beyond the bank where she stood, the land dipped down into a little hollow that couldn't be seen from the road. There in the hollow was a portable shed not much bigger than a garden shed. It had probably been overlooked by a highway crew when they left because it was invisible from the road and half-hidden by scattered willows, birches and pines.

The shed door was locked but a small high sliding window looked as if it wasn't quite closed. It was too small for anyone but Frankie to squeeze through. She hopped up and down trying to reach it. "Too high," she puffed. "Need something to stand on." She looked at the bike lying in the grass. "If I leaned it against the wall, I might be able to balance on the seat. Hmmm. Tricky. Maybe as a last resort." She poked around the perimeter of the shed. In the back was a huge wooden spool. It looked like it had been used for the piece of cable that was lying in the grass next to it. The spool was the right height. She tried to push it over so she could roll it around to the window. It only wobbled. She stood back and pushed the hair out of her eyes , then hunkered down and pushed, grunting, "The legs. Are. The. Strongest. Part of the body ... Ooof ...

"Ta da!" Frankie bowed and nodded to Dan and her imaginary audience as she had seen her dad do in his happy moods. Then she rolled the spool around to the front of the shed. Getting it upright wasn't any picnic. She had to crouch really low and ended up falling over the spool as it righted and rolling onto the grass. She lay there looking up at the stars. Dan rushed over to lick her nose like he always did when she got down to his level.

It was nice on the grass. Tempting to just fall asleep. But she hauled herself up and clambered onto the spool. The window was now chest height and slid open easily. It was a squeeze getting in, and once she was through she found herself standing on her head on a table under the window. She carefully lowered herself, pulling her legs into a crouch before crawling down to the floor. Then she opened the door from the inside and Dan rushed in as if they'd been separated for days. With the door open there was enough light from the moon to see a couple of chairs and a cot, a watercooler with a few inches of water left and a cupboard empty except for three mugs and a spoon. Frankie wheeled the bike in and got out the food she'd filched from the cycle-tour buffet. She and Dan drank some water and shared the food, then cuddled together on the cot under his blanket. She wondered sleepily how her dad was doing and thought about how Augusta still missed her mother even though she was an old lady. With a pang, Frankie realized she was having trouble remembering her own mother's smile. But she remembered the way it felt.

The moon rose higher and, framed in the little window, kept her company. The crickets sang and so did the frogs. The wind whistled an accompaniment as it blew through the trees and the tin eaves of the shed.

There's a hazy rainbow haloing the moon
And diamonds someone's scattered
Across the sky so dark and blue
Wisps of silver cloud drift like spangled gauze
Do you look down and see me?
I only ask because
I miss you more than anything, your voice, your eyes, your hair
Until the night reminds me that you are everywhere

Every evening breeze is your caress
The rustle of the leaves is the rustle of your dress
The stars' glint is the sparkle in your eyes
The moon is your heart glowing for me
I feel it deep inside

Coyote's call and cricket's song
They're singing with your lullaby
I can hear it now so clearly
As sleep comes now to steal me
I feel your hand in mine
My face pillowed on your breast
The whispered breeze croons softly,
"Good night, my love,
Sweet Rest."

Chapter Fourteen

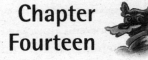

The morning air was so fresh it was like some kind of amazing, intoxifying gas.

"This is surprising," thought Frankie, breathing in big lungfuls. "I thought air was just a bunch of nothing." But this was *substantial*, like a nutritious substance. It made her skin feel clean even though she hadn't had a bath. It made waking up a very exciting thing to do. She stepped out of the shed into sparkling sun and birdsong. Dan got very frisky and ran around sniffing and peeing on at least seventeen different clumps of grass, rocks and short tufty shrubs. He stopped dead, riveted by an anthill, then barked down a gopher hole, before charging a couple of strutting crows. Frankie stood with her hands on her hips, feeling immensely strong and capable. She also felt extremely hungry and thirsty, so she dug out the remains of the purloined provisions and shared them with Dan.

Then she wheeled Hippogriff out of the shed and they got started again.

Soon Frankie came to a village and she decided to stop for food at a small grocery store. The store had a wooden screen door which banged behind her. Her feet clomped on the worn wood floors. She could see that both door and floors used to be painted turquoise. The man behind the counter was reading a newspaper and didn't seem to notice Dan trailing around after her as she looked up and down the aisles. She was used to shopping in corner stores, choosing the food for her meals, so she knew where to look for things. Little stores always arranged things the same way — fruits and vegetables by the window, milk and eggs and margarine in the dairy case by the wall and aisles of stuff in cans and boxes. This one also had packaged sandwiches and salads in the cooler next to the cold drinks, so she bought one of each and other provisions to keep her strength up: cookies, a carton of milk, a box of juice, an apple, a banana, and Milkbones for Dan. There was a big, cold ice-cream case. She looked up at the clock on the wall. It was only 9 a.m.

"Can I have an ice cream?" She stood in front of the storekeeper. He looked up from his paper.

"As long as you got money to pay for it, you can have anything you want."

Frankie bought a double-decker vanilla and strawberry with chocolate chips. She couldn't stop smiling as she ate it outside.

The village had long ago dwindled to a picturesque

huddle behind Frankie and Dan when *Pffft!* the front tire went flat,

"Hippogriff, don't fail me now!" Frankie said, feeling confident all would be well, but the tire stayed flat. "Hippogriff, don't fail me now," she said again, louder this time.

"Are you talking to the bike?" came a voice behind her. She whipped around and saw a boy with curly, curly hair and freckles over the world's smallest nose. Knobby knees stuck out of a pair of baggy shorts.

"This tire's flat and I don't know how to fix it." Seeing the boy's amused eyes, Frankie protested, "I'm only ten!"

The boy came closer and crouched down to inspect the wheel. He looked up at her with long-lashed green eyes flecked with gold and Frankie saw with a start that the person she thought was a boy was a girl!

"I've got a patch kit at home. I'll go get it." And the girl ran off like the wind across the field to a house in a copse of poplars set against a haze of blue hills.

Seconds later a dot came flying out of the house and hurtled towards Frankie. Panting, the girl flopped down on the grass and offered Frankie a bottle of water.

"I'm Dilly," she said.

"You're what?"

"Dilly, short for Desdemona."

"I'm Frankie —"

"— And you're just short."

"Ha, ha."

Dilly took Hippogriff's front wheel off and pulled out the nail that had caused the puncture.

"There's the culprit!" She showed Frankie how to mark the spot with a yellow crayon, take the tire off the rim, and how to roughen the surface of the tire to make a good bond between the glue and the patch. Then, puffing, Dilly hauled a big smooth rock over to use as a weight on the patch while the glue was drying.

As they waited, Frankie and Dilly ate the cookies Frankie had just bought and drank the milk, now a little warm. Then Frankie pulled open the carton and poured the rest of Dilly's water into it for Dan.

"I'm home sick from school," said Dilly.

"You don't look sick to me."

"I am," she said and made a pathetic face, then laughed and rolled over in the grass. She told Frankie the names of the wildflowers growing in the grass next to them. "That's Purple Vetch and that's Indian Paintbrush." She found a tiny wild strawberry for Frankie to sample.

They wandered along the edge of the road as Dilly pointed out this plant and that. She pounced on one plant, declaring, "And this'll make you sleep if you make tea out of it." She snatched a handful of leaves and gave them to Frankie. "It's wild hops." Frankie put the hops into her pocket. She was amazed at all the things Dilly knew and could do.

Finally it was time to put the tire's inner tube back on and pump a little air into it. Frankie and Dilly took turns standing on the pump and jumping up and down. It was easier getting the tire back on than it had been getting it off. Then more air. Puff puff. It took forever and the tire didn't seem to be getting hard enough. Finally they gave up. It would just have to do. Dilly instructed Frankie to stop at the next gas station for air.

"I'll ride with you a ways," offered Dilly, and after a wobbling start, Frankie sat on the seat with her legs dangling and Dilly stood up and pedalled. They screamed down a winding hill, Dan barking insanely and happily all the way.

At the bottom, Dilly got off. "I've got to go now," she said, touching Frankie's arm before swinging at some long grass and running off across the field. She turned once and waved, hopping up and down, comically sticklike and floppy like a freckled, smiling marionette.

"Good luck! Good luck! Good luck! See you in the movies!" And turning again, Dilly threw herself into a chaotic cartwheel, then ran off across the field towards home.

Francesca watched until she disappeared, feeling a little lonely ache of her heart as it pulled after Dilly. Then, with a sigh, got on the bike and started off down the road. She looked down at her newly patched tire and wondered if it was too soft to make it to the next gas station. But the tire was firm and sound as if it had newly been filled with air. Strange. Did the bike mean for her to stop and meet Dilly? If so, it now meant for her to carry on her way.

Chapter
Fifteen

"It's him from next door." Violet turned away from Ron at the front door and hollered up the stairs to Augusta. "So soon? You'd better send him up."

Ron was a little put-out by this greeting. They shouted past him as if he wasn't there. Stony-faced, Violet opened the door wider to let him in. Ron puffed up the stairs and into Augusta's bedroom. "I've come to take Frankie out for breakfast." Catching his breath, he peered around, thinking, *This really is the most astonishing bedroom.* He looked over the paintings, bronze figurines and framed photographs, the carved mantelpiece and the books, books, books everywhere.

Ron was excited. He was dying to tell Frankie his good news. He'd woken up this morning clear-headed for the first time in months, possibly years.

"I've sent her to tennis camp," Augusta responded, blurting out the first thing that came into her head. She suddenly realized she should have been prepared with a story.

"Tennis camp? Does Frankie play tennis?" Had he really not noticed a tennis racket? "Well, how long is that for? And where is it? What's it going to cost me?"

"A week. It's for a week. And it'll cost nothing, nothing. It was already paid for. Non-refundable. A lovely place. It's ... it's ... now, where is it? Oh yes, I know, it's out in the country ... near the village of Pigglestop! That's it." Augusta sank back into her chair. At least it was only a partial lie. Zelda's hotel on the lake really was near Pigglestop.

Ron frowned. There was nothing he could say, could he? Still he felt disappointed — shocked, actually — to have Frankie zipped off to camp like that.

"I really, really appreciate everything you're doing for Frankie, Augusta, but shouldn't you have asked me? I know I'm not much of a parent, but I'm still her father." Ron tried not to pout.

"You were out!" Augusta gambled. "My lawyer's son suddenly came down with mumps and he offered his place at camp to Francesca. My lawyer needed an immediate decision. I'm dreadfully sorry. I should have consulted you, I know. Please forgive me."

"Oh, of course." Ron felt ungrateful and embarrassed. "Of course, that's fine."

"Have they come yet to take her away?"

Ron gawked. "They?"

"Social Services." *Really, the man's mind is going,* Augusta thought. "That woman from Social Services was here yesterday. You weren't here when she came."

"I know. I got cold feet, but I overcame it and got back just as she was getting into her car. She came in and we talked. She ended up giving me a week to get my act together."

"A week? Excellent, excellent!" Augusta felt a pang of guilt over sending Frankie off unneccessarily, but quickly shook it off. She wasn't used to doubting her own judgements.

"You know," Ron continued, "I need to get the house in order, buy groceries, stop drinking ..." He mumbled the last bit.

"Speak up! I can't hear you."

"STOP DRINKING!" he shouted.

"And about time, too."

Ron sighed, rubbing his head fiercely, sending his hair into crazy tufts. "I know, I know." He was starting to deflate. And he'd had such a good day yesterday. All those agencies, appointments and meetings. He tried to focus. "But since she's gone off to tennis camp —"

"Clean up the house, you say?" Augusta interrupted, struggling to keep the conversation off the fictional tennis camp.

"It'll be a huge job," Ron admitted. "Frankie doesn't even have a proper bedroom."

"Mrs. Slatternly's an excellent cleaner. I'll lend her to you for a couple of days."

At the foot of the stairs, a dish shattered loudly.

"Everything all right down there, Mrs. Slatternly?"

"Yes, Missus H." Violet sank onto the bottom step, where she'd been drying a plate and eavesdropping. The thought of actual physical labour made her feel exhausted.

Ron peered more closely at the bedroom, really seeing it for the first time. Mrs. Slatternly was a cleaning lady? But the house was filthy! Something was definitely fishy here. Then he noticed a cheque on Augusta's tray. To stall for time, he said, "Writing Mrs. Slatternly's paycheque, Augusta?"

"Oh no. This is for the grocer."

Ron was no expert at reading upsidedown, but he could plainly see the $50 cheque wasn't made out to Everfresh Grocers but to Mrs. V. Slatternly. "Does she deposit the cheques into her own account, then pay the bills in cash?" he asked, hoping for an innocent explanation.

"Never! I hope I know better how to run my household. One shouldn't put temptation in the way of one's servants, don't you agree?"

"Well, I don't have much experience of servants, but I know temptation. I've yielded to it often enough."

"Ha ha! Ah yes, 'I can resist everything except temptation,'" Augusta quoted Oscar Wilde.

Ron was only half-listening. He was busy staring around the room, at the dust and gauzy grey wisps in the corners of the ceiling, the ragged lace of the curtains, the tea-stained counterpane and the ash-choked grate. "What is Mrs. Slatternly's rate for cleaning, then, Augusta?"

"Highway robbery!" insisted Augusta, but when she quoted the sum Ron was shocked at the miserable low wage. He wondered what he should say but before he could formulate another thought, Augusta rang her bell and shouted, "Mrs. Slatternly, could you come upstairs?"

Violet came through the doorway, then stopped abruptly and grew pale when she saw her cheque still in plain view. Her frightened eyes slid to Ron. He just looked back at her with no expression at all while Augusta said grandly, "Mrs. Slatternly, would you be so kind as to do some cleaning for Mr. Rudderless this afternoon? After lunch, I should think. Your usual scandalous rate, of course."

Violet was perspiring. She mopped at her face and neck with the damp dishtowel. "Yes, fine, Missus H." She started out of the room.

"You've forgotten the cheque!" Augusta felt for the edges of the rectangle of paper, then scrawled her signature. "Drop that off on your way home, would you?"

Her face miserable, Violet swooped back into the room, snatched the incriminating cheque and fled down the stairs.

Ron returned home feeling deflated and lonely. He wandered around his house picking things up and putting them away, shocked at its disorder. No wonder the social worker had freaked out. He started moving his broken instruments and radios, tools and parts down to the basement workbench. It was covered with empties, so he had to move all those somewhere else. He stood with a cardboard box full of three broken euphoniums in his arms, turning in circles, looking for a bare spot in the junk-filled basement, almost whimpering with confusion. But after a couple of hours he'd found a place for most of the instruments and created a workshop area.

Wearily, he dragged himself up the stairs, clinging to the banister, then sagged into a kitchen chair. As he sat, Ron tried to imagine Frankie at tennis camp with a lot of rich kids. "I hope she's having a nice time, Germ." The mottled cat leapt onto his lap. He looked around. The kitchen was a horror. The sight of it made him want to run out to the nearest bar. Then he remembered the advice he'd received at his support group the night before: "Don't get tired, don't get hungry"; "first things first"; and "KISS — Keep It Simple, Stupid." He smiled half-heartedly, sighing as he got up to make himself some lunch. "I'll go to another support group meeting tonight." There was one somewhere in town several times a day, seven days a week.

Ron was just starting on his baloney sandwich and mug of tea when the doorbell rang. He opened the door and Violet threw herself onto his unsuspecting body.

"Please don't report me to the police, Mr. Rudderless," she wailed. "I'll give the money back somehow. I promise."

Ron staggered backwards under the weight of the sobbing woman. "No one's calling the police. Let's just sit down and have a nice cup of tea and a talk. You call me Ron and I'll call you Violet and we'll figure this out."

A half hour later, over tea, a much calmer Violet confided, "I've known Missus H since God was in diapers. She was a young Canadian lodging in my mother's house in East London during the war."

"Really?" exclaimed Ron, astonished.

"You'd never know it to hear Mrs. La di da Halberton-Ffrench talk now, would you? She was twenty and I was ten. When she joined up I thought she was so beautiful and brave in her uniform. Later I worked for her as general dogsbody when she had an art gallery on the King's Road in Chelsea, helping with framing and packaging, serving at parties. She was so glamorous. She was a photographer then, surrounded by famous friends — artists and writers and the like. She even wrote poetry that was published in little magazines. Well, I got married and moved up north. We exchanged Christmas cards and eventually she moved back to Canada. My husband was as useful as a fart in a hat, excuse my French! Fell off a ladder putting in a light bulb and that was the end of him. After he died, my brother talked me into emigrating to Canada. I wrote to Augusta and she said to call in when I arrived.

"I was shocked when I saw her, I can tell you. She was nearly blind, all alone. No cameras, no glamorous friends or parties. She never married, you know. She was too independent. High standards when it came to men. No one was good enough for her, though many tried. So she was all alone with no one to take care of her. She has a sister with pots of money, but Missus H wants nothing to do with her. A falling out over their mother's ring. Stupid reason if you ask me, but you know how sisters can be."

"Is Augusta poor, then?"

"Oh no. She's not rich, mind. But she's quite comfortable, though you'd never know it, she's such a penny pincher. It kills her to let go of a dime. I'm not allowed to throw anything out. Though I do. She checks up on me. Makes me save the tinfoil and wash the plastic bags."

"So is that why you write cheques to yourself?" Ron poured her another cup of tea.

Violet reddened and looked down at her hands. "My pension wouldn't feed a mouse. I asked her for a raise, but she just ranted on about being sent into the poorhouse. When I was caught short for my rent, I just wrote myself a cheque. It's wrong, I know. But it's never much. Thirty-five dollars here, $50 there. Never more than that. I can't live on what she pays me."

"But Violet, you don't do anything. Augusta's house is appalling."

Violet sat up, indignant. "Steady on there, chum. I make her meals. I do the shopping. I make her bed, do the laundry, wash the dishes, feed the animals, take her abuse. I beg to differ. She gets what she pays for, she does."

"It sounds like you hate her."

"Hate her!" Violet was shocked. "Hate Missus H? I'm ... I'm ... well, to put it plain — I love the old tyrant. I could have strangled her when she didn't let me know she was out of hospital."

"But how can you say you love someone if you don't take good care of them —" Ron stopped, mortified when he realized what he was saying. "I'm sorry. I'm the last person who should be asking such a question."

Violet reached over and patted his hand. "Don't worry, love. I'll help you tidy up. It's what I'm here for."

"You and I have got to reform, Violet."

"Well, off your bum, chum. Let's get this rubbish cleaned up. And I'll give up my life of crime. Just when I was getting so good at it, too!"

Chapter
Sixteen

Miles and miles went by, but riding the bike didn't
seem to tire Frankie. The hills were a little harder
but even when they were so steep they seemed to go
straight up, she only had to strain a little. And Dan and
Hippogriff always managed to find a side road or a
country lane, even though most of them didn't seem to
match Augusta's disintegrating map. Dan would point
his nose and bark and the Hippogriff would agree or
refuse to go down certain roads. Frankie bought things to
eat at roadside stands or stores and stopped at a gas
station to fill up her water bottle and use the washroom.
She tried to be careful with her money, realizing it wasn't
very much. Also, she was worried about not showing up
at Mary's house, where she'd been expected last night.
She went to the phone booth and called the number
Augusta had given her for Mary, but there was no answer.

The sun shone and the leaves on the roadside trees waved and fluttered. Frankie sang a lot. Dan joined in at the bits in his range. Even though he didn't know the words, he was good with a soulful "Woo woo."

By late morning, they were riding along a frontage road beside the highway on the outskirts of a town, past car dealerships, drive-in burger franchises, jumbo home improvement stores and strip malls. Frankie told Dan the story of her life. "... And after the German measles, I got the mumps. Then after the mumps, I got chicken pox which prevented me from getting my Guppies swim badge. But then I got Pickles, my best friend ..."

She didn't notice a car slowing down behind them. A man with a smile like a crocodile talked to himself as he watched the little girl in overall shorts and a T-shirt pedalling all by herself.

"What do we have here?" he purred to himself. "Another convert to my merry little band of thieves?" He pulled alongside, leaned across the front seat and called out the window, "Excuse me, miss, I wonder if you could direct me to Carnival Street?"

Frankie turned and looked to see who was talking to her. A shiver prickled her arms and the back of her neck. Dan growled softly from his basket and a tooth showed dangerously from beneath his curled black lip. Frankie found it hard to speak but thought it would be rude not to answer the man's question. "I don't know that street. I don't live here."

"Ooh ... you don't, eh? Well, look, why don't you hop in? We'll put your bike in the trunk and I'll give you a ride to wherever you're going?" The car was going very slowly and was edging over so close that Frankie wobbled a bit with confusion and nerves. The man had one hand on the steering wheel and was leaning way across the seat, straining to get closer.

The gap between the car and the curb became ever narrower and any second now she'd have to stop and get off the bike if she didn't want to fall over or be crushed. The man smiled his crocodile smile and reached his long arm out the window to touch her shoulder. *Snap!* Dan's little teeth grazed the big veiny hand, leaving red lines.

"Why you ...!" The man let go of the wheel and lunged across the seat to strike Dan.

Dan went flying with a yelp. The man lurched back to grab the steering wheel again and Frankie cried out, "Hippogriff, don't fail me now!" The bike leapt the curb and wheeled around so fast and so low it was leaning sideways into the curve. Frankie reached down and scooped up Dan as they spun round. Then the bike zoomed upright as they shot off in the opposite direction and bounced back down onto the road. Her legs were going so fast to keep up with the speeding bike, they were a blur beneath her.

The man slammed the car to a stop and reversed, turning awkwardly in the narrow road. He stepped on the accelerator and roared up beside them again, still grinning. "Hey! Slow down. Sorry I lost my temper there. I'm really very nice. I just want to talk to you about an excellent business opportunity."

Frankie's heart was pounding. Dan's ears lay flat against his head from in the wind and his brown eyes bulged. He turned to snarl and bark at the man, leaping to the edge of his basket and practically falling out in his eagerness to get his teeth into him.

"Sit back, Dan," Frankie begged as they passed the turnoff from the highway where they'd first come onto the side road. The car blocked them from turning out again. Ahead there was a checkered yellow diamond sign and a chain link fence. Dead end.

"Oh, Hippogriff don't fail me now!" pleaded Frankie.

Still going full tilt, as if it was going to crash head-on into the fence, the bike leapt the curb, and leaning low sideways like a ballplayer skidding into home plate, Frankie, Dan and the bike slid towards the fence where a section near the ground had been slashed open and bent back. Frankie heard the car door slam and feet running as they scraped under the fence. Then, springing upright again, Frankie, Dan and Hippogriff tobogganed headlong down a rocky, scrubby slope to a parking lot full of buses. It was a teeth-jarring descent — *Yelp! Yelp! Yelp!*, and the agonized squeal of springs, dog and girl — until they flew off the curb at the bottom and swerved to a skidding halt behind a driver loading bikes onto a rack at the back of a bus.

"This is the last one," the driver announced as he turned and picked up Hippogriff. He strode to the front and Frankie hurried after him. She slowed down just enough to read the sign in the window. It said: "Department of Highways Free Tunnel Shuttle."

The driver said, "You can't bring that dog on the bus."

"What dog?"

"That dog that was in your bike basket."

"Oh, he's gone home," replied Frankie, hauling herself

up the stairs and nearly strangling from the weight in her pack. The doors closed with an enormous hydraulic sigh and the bus wheeled out of the parking lot and onto the highway.

"You're very dirty for a little girl," said a woman in the front seat.

"Yes, I know. It's worrying. I hope to grow out of it."

The woman nodded in somber agreement and Frankie continued down the aisle, swaying and clutching at the backs of seats until she tumbled into an empty place. She held the zippered Dan on her lap, bent down and whispered, "Then after chicken pox, I got appendicitis ..." She looked up to the top of the hill they'd just hurtled down. The crocodile man was staring down at her through the chain link fence as they drove past.

Chapter Seventeen

R on nervously tapped his baton on the music stand but no one paid any attention. He was substitute directing the afternoon Seniors' Swing Band. Ron was surprised at how badly behaved seniors were. They were wandering around the room, clapping each other on the shoulder in greeting, gossiping, shrieking with laughter and generally carrying on as if it was a party. He tapped again and called for order, but couldn't make himself heard above the genial uproar. He turned around, picked up his euphonium and blared an ear-splitting reveille. Shocked silence.

"Who're you?" one of them hollered.

"My name is Ron Rudderless. I will be your director while Frank is away. As you probably know, his wife is expecting a baby at any time now."

"Boy or girl?"

"She hasn't had it yet, as far as I know."

"I have a new grandchild," a lady clarinetist in a hat called out.

"So do I!" cried the tuba. And pretty soon every senior in the room was enumerating their descendants.

This was getting out of hand. Ron tapped on the music stand. No response. He suddenly realized that at least two-thirds of the room were wearing hearing aids. They couldn't hear him! Oh brother! He cupped his hands around his mouth and shouted, "We'll start with 'Little Brown Jug' please."

The seniors were all talking at once, but Ron finally got them started. He found no one watched his baton except for the bassoon. The old men in the clarinet section and the lady with the hat hid behind their music stands. Below the stands he could see feet tapping to different rhythms. He gestured for the musicians to stop but most of them just kept going. He shouted back to the drummer, who seemed to be playing something Latin, "Could you follow my beat, please?"

"You're doing it wrong," the drummer asserted.

"Typical arrogant drummer," Ron muttered to himself.

"I heard that!"

Uh oh. This one wasn't wearing a hearing aid. "Could you lower your stands, please, so you can watch me," Ron addressed the headless band. There was a chorus of protest.

"I can't. I have trifocals."

"What do I have to see you for?"

Ron was surprised. "Well, uh, so you'll know when to start, for one thing."

"Oh, I just start when everyone else does."

When rehearsal finally ended, Ron had a hoarse throat and was sure they all hated him. "There goes my new job," he said as he packed up his music. But when he looked up, the seniors were crowded around, telling him what a terrific young man he was. Young? Terrific?

A little while later, Ron fell into the house carrying his euphonium case, his briefcase overflowing with music, and three bags of groceries. Quivering with exhaustion, he wanted not one drink but ten. "I don't think I can do this," he thought. "This is too hard." He tried bargaining with himself. "Maybe I can quit drinking next week, once I've got everything done." But the little voice in his head said, *Don't get tired. Don't get hungry.*

With trembling hands Ron put on the kettle and made himself a peanut butter and banana sandwich. He bit and chewed, took a slurp of tea and sighed with satisfaction. "That's better. I may live after all."

He looked at the clock. "Time to make peace." He headed over to Augusta's. While he stood on the porch waiting to be let in, he looked around at the peeling paint and the sagging, buckling porch steps. The veranda was dark under an overgrown wisteria that hung down from the porch roof in big purple clusters. He could hear Augusta's little bell ringing, Augusta shouting down and Violet shouting up that she was coming. Violet opened the door mid-shout.

"Who is it?" came Augusta's voice.

"Ron," Violet called up in return.

"That's Mr. Rudderless to you, Mrs. Slatternly!" came the aristocratic reprimand.

Violet turned to Ron. "See what I have to put up with?"

As he stepped inside, Ron could smell soap and furniture polish.

"I've never cleaned so much in me blessed life," Violet added.

Grinning, Ron gave Violet the thumbs-up sign and started up the stairs.

"I don't know what's gotten into Mrs. Slatternly." Augusta was in a good mood. "She's vacuuming and I can smell furniture polish. She turfed me out of bed and changed my sheets. What did you do? Hypnotize her?"

"We had a talk, Augusta." Augusta was up and dressed and sitting with Harold the cat on her lap in her big chair beside the fireplace. Ron could see that the grate had been swept clean. He crossed the room and sat in a small wicker armchair by the window. A soft breeze alternately pulled and blew the lace curtains. "About how neither of us is taking proper care of the ones we love best."

"Try not to spout nonsense, Ron. Francesca is your daughter. Mrs. Slatternly is my daily."

"I would have thought that someone you've known since you were twenty might be called an old friend. She told me about how beautiful and brave you were when you were young. How upset she was to not be here when you got out of the hospital. How fond she is of you."

"Fond! She acts like she hates me. Her meals are swill and all she does is complain." Augusta was clutching the cat so tightly, he yowled and jumped down.

"And you don't pay her enough to live on or treat her with any respect. If you don't like her why don't you fire her and hire somebody else?"

"How dare you!" Augusta was not used to being talked to like that. The nerve! The ingratitude! But curiosity got the better of her. "She really said I was brave and beautiful?"

"She did. And she told me how glamorous and surrounded by friends you were."

Augusta smiled to herself. Harold jumped back up onto her lap. "I suppose I should dismiss her, but, well, I have known her for most of my life. I might be a little fond of her, as horrible as she is."

"She said the same of you. In fact, she said she loved you. And is worried about you."

"Love! Ridiculous! She's plotting something."

Ron wondered for a moment if all the tears from Violet had been a con job. He didn't think so. It didn't feel that way in his gut.

"Augusta, you need to double Violet's pay," Ron said firmly.

Augusta recoiled in horror. "Are you out of your tiny mind?" Furious, she pushed herself up from the chair, dumping Harold onto the floor. "I can't afford that!"

"Yes, you can!" Ron continued boldly. "And if you do, I can guarantee it won't end up costing you."

"What do you mean?" Augusta asked suspiciously.

Uh-oh, he'd said too much. "I mean..." Then inspiration struck. "You could ask her to live here. You'd receive twenty-four-hour care and she wouldn't have to pay rent!"

By the time Ron left for his support group they'd agreed on the new terms. Violet came upstairs and happily accepted the proposal to move in and the small raise. She also promised to improve the meals. And both Violet and Augusta agreed they would talk more respectfully to each other.

Chapter Eighteen

The shuttle pulled into the loop and unloaded its passengers, luggage and bicycles. There was a line of people waiting to go back the other way. Frankie pushed her bike to the edge of the of the lot and waited until the bus driver had driven off. Dan erupted from the backpack like a geyser, yipping and spinning in circles he was so overjoyed to get out. Frankie looked up to see the disapproving lady wheeling up with her bicycle.

"I see you're selective with the truth as well as dirty." She nodded meaningfully at Dan.

Frankie glanced down at Dan worriedly. Could the lady report them to the bus authorities? But then she noticed the lady was smiling.

"Very wise under the circumstances," said the lady. "Stupid rule, in my opinion."

"Sure is," agreed Frankie, surprised.

"You must be Francesca. I'm Mary, Augusta's friend, and any friend of Augusta's is a friend of mine." She put out her hand. "I just had this feeling that if I started out, I'd meet you. I wasn't sure it was you on the bus, but when I saw you with Hippogriff and Dan, I knew."

Frankie felt like falling into Mary's arms. Instead, she pumped Mary's hand up and down in happy relief. "Oh, I'm so glad to see you, Mary." Hot food! A safe place to sleep! In short, a friend. They got on their bikes and started down the road.

"You sound like someone who thinks for herself," Mary observed. "I like to speak my mind myself."

Frankie wasn't sure about that. "Doesn't speaking your mind just make people mad?"

"Quite possibly. But Francesca, you might as well learn this now. If somebody somewhere isn't mad at you, then you're nothing more than a spineless worm — a human custard, quivering in fear of opening your mouth in case someone else disapproves. It's a wonderful thing to have a mind of your own. Never be ashamed of it. It doesn't hurt to take a bath once in a while, though. You might find you make friends more easily if you do."

Mary was wearing a pink blouse with blue rosebud buttons down the front, a voluminous skirt and sturdy sandals. She filled her lungs with air and sat up straight, grandly looking around with a big smile. "Isn't cycling marvelous?" Mary's bike was almost as old as Frankie's. "The most efficient mode of movement in the universe."

Soon they came to a lane marked by a sign that read "Blue Spruce Cottage: Sanctuary For Animal Friends In Need."

"This is it," Mary said. Dan jumped down and ran ahead.

⌣

Spruce Cottage was a pretty little house nearly buried in white rambling roses and purple clematis vines. Three blue spruces stood behind it, friendly giants making a lovely background to red poppies, irises, sweetpeas, honeysuckle, roses, forget-me-nots and gorgeous blue spikes of larkspur and delphinium. Chickens, ducks and geese flapped and pecked up and down the paths — crazy paving of crockery, stone, brick and slate — and disappeared into the shrubbery.

"Oh, it's lovely!" Frankie had never seen such a house. She decided then and there that one day she would live in a house just like it.

They dismounted and wheeled their bikes around the back. Everywhere she looked, Frankie saw animals. In a small paddock a limping mother deer with her fawn shared space with two goats. In another paddock a llama chewed and stared at them. In pens and ponds around the property Mary showed her otters and magpies, a wounded eagle and a coyote, raccoons and a bobcat. "People bring the wounded animals they find. Or sometimes animals they don't want anymore, like that llama there. Sometimes animals just come on their own. I guess something tells them they'll be taken care of here." Woods surrounded the property. A section of the forest had been enclosed with twelve-foot-high chainlink fencing wound through the trees. In it, an elderly bear with a grey muzzle and a leg in a cast snoozed in a patch of dappled sunlight.

"That's Terry. He's got a broken leg. I'm a retired people doctor, but I seem to be taking care of animals now. Let's go have some lunch." Mary led the way through a small kitchen garden of herbs and vegetables. Fruit trees and berry bushes crowded back the forest. So much in such a compact spot. The air was scented with rosemary and strawberries.

In the kitchen on the floor a skunk in a cushioned basket opened its eyes sleepily. It tilted its head back, stretching its neck to gaze at Mary.

"This is Maurice Ravel. He's my sweetheart. He's very sick so he's here in the intensive ward." But you're going to get better, aren't you darling?" Mary knelt and stroked his head. Frankie looked around at the kitchen/intensive ward. Under the table in a cardboard box sat a forlorn-looking rabbit with a bandaged ear and a bare patch on his back showing recent stitches. And on the counter was a crow with a bandaged foot. He was examining them with bright intelligent eyes. Mary stood up. "That's Cecil down there. A narrow escape from a predator. And Eric here lost two toes in a brawl, but that's crows for you. They're both recovering from surgery.

"Now, I'll show you where you're sleeping tonight, then we'll have lunch. And then ..." Mary rubbed her hands together gleefully, "I'd like to take you to something very special — a very unique bicycle fair."

Mary served a lunch of creamy corn chowder with warm cheese biscuits delicious with melting butter. After, they had fragrant black currant and mint tea, and strawberry pie. While they ate, Mary told Frankie about her friendship with Augusta.

"She was very brave in the war. She never considered not doing something because she was frightened. She just went ahead driving that ambulance through war zones or down strange roads in the middle of the night. I think that's why it didn't seem strange to her to send you off on your own. Also never having had children, I suspect she just sees them as short grownups. She might not realize how small you are. Or how the world has changed. But Augusta is also brilliant. She would have been a great photographer if she hadn't lost her eyesight. She has that heightened intuition and perception that great artists have. It borders on psychic power. She judged you would be able to do this and also that it was the best thing for you and everyone connected to you. She thought it was the right moment. But my question is: Are you sure you want to do this, Francesca? You don't have to continue on this journey. You can just stay here with me and help with the animals for as long as you like."

Frankie thought carefully before saying, "I love it here. When I grow up I want to have a home just like it. But I have to do this trip. I'm not alone. I have Dan and the Hippogriff. The day before I left, it felt like there were two paths. One was to wait for the social worker to maybe take me away to more houses and different schools. And the other was to do this for Augusta. Sometimes it's scary but other times I'm so happy. It feels like I need to ride the bike and find the ring. I feel like if I do that, everything will turn out."

Mary listened to the small red-headed girl speak with such thoughtfulness and resolution. Moved and impressed, she said, "I can see why Augusta thinks you're so special." Frankie closed her eyes and pulled her ears, pleased and embarrassed.

"I can see that the best thing I can do is to help you in any way I can," Mary continued. "Augusta asked me to tell you more about the bike. I'll tell you everything I know.

"The Hippogriff has become something different from what Curious and Patrick thought they were making. It can do more and less than they thought it could. On the one hand, it is more than an electrical phenomenon. I think that's because the Human Responsive Metal was fashioned into a bicycle which is in itself a sort of miracle. I've been thinking about how to explain it to you ever since Augusta told me you were coming." She went to the bookcase and pulled out a book. Opening it at a flagged page, she read: "Many philosophers of technology and society believe the bicycle is one of the highest forms of technology ... Some have even described the bicycle as the martyred saint of the machine age." She closed the book.

"I think through some miracle, because the extraordinary machine that is the bicycle was combined with Human Responsive Metals, the Hippogriff became a creature, a hugely sympathetic one. As children, Zelda and Augusta tried to explain to the two metallurgists what magic they had produced. But they were young men looking for immediate practical results. They were completely focussed on military and industrial applications that could give them fame and fortune. They didn't want to be lumped in with spiritualists and crystal ball readers — the lunatic fringe. They thought they'd be laughed at.

They were scientists and had no use for metals that responded to immeasurable qualities like intuition and psychic glimmerings. So they ignored Augusta and Zelda, and the children went on to experiment with Hippogriff and to discover qualities the grownups didn't value or ignored.

"I'll show you. Come outside." Mary wheeled Hippogriff to the very end of her property. She got on the bike then leaned forward and very quietly said, "Bike, take me home."

Hippogriff's handlebars raised up until they were no longer the same height as the seat but much higher. Then, on either side, the handlebars bent inward from hidden hinges so that the handlebars now formed a triangle. In the very middle of the handlebars, the cap under the Hippogriff sculpture started to spin upwards, telescoping out of the hollow stem that connected to the fork holding the front wheel. It spun until it was eight inches high. Still turning, this centre tube opened out into a flat tongue and folded down toward Mary. It became a head rest, just wide enough to lay your cheek against. The whole thing was now the right height for Mary to rest her arms and then rest her head between them, which she did. The Hippogriff ornament was curled under so it wouldn't poke Mary once she laid her head down. The bike shimmered and as soon as Mary raised both feet onto the pedals, it lifted off the ground and whooshed gently down the yard to land on Mary's back porch.

Frankie ran up breathlessly, her heart fluttering, just in time to see the handlebars smoothly resuming their original shape. "It flew! It actually flew."

"Yes. If you are injured or ill the bike will take you home. Usually it will only fly if you are physically unable to ride. But Hippogriff and I are old friends." Mary stroked the worn leather seat. "It understood I needed to show you what it could do."

"Why didn't Augusta tell me?"

"She may not know. When she went to England for all those years, she left the bike with me. She told me what she knew about it, and what she guessed. I was a young medical student then, but I was always interested in sympathetic energy fields. It's part of many other healing traditions. So I kept riding the bike and experimenting with its powers.

"I think the bike is actually repelling the ground — a kind of reverse magnetism. It is responding to your psychic need. And the greater the need, the greater the response. Like I said, it is a very sympathetic creature."

⌣ ⋅

"Human-Powered Vehicle Fair" read the sign by the side of the road.

"I am so happy you came today," Mary told Frankie later that afternoon as she led the way down a narrow side road overhung by tall buddleia bushes. "It is so lucky — or maybe not luck. It might be fate, that you are here when this fair is on."

The hot still air above them danced with butterflies and buzzed with bees. Nodding pink spirea leaned over wild roses, and flowering red currant bushes dangled their pink and white blossoms like earrings. In the shady water of the ditch, waterbugs skated around huge yellow skunk cabbages and wild irises. Ahead they could see other people travelling on the road and before long they were riding among eight-foot-high tricycles. Then zooming past came a couple of "recumbent bikes," as Mary called them. One driver was lying on his back on his bike and pedalling, the other one was lying on her stomach. There were tandems of two, three, four and five riders all in a row on the same long bikes. Then came an astonishing circular bike with seats set all around the frame. On it sat seven men in business suits all pedalling, all arguing at the top of their lungs. The only thing that kept them from crashing into the ditch was the one man facing forward, wearing goggles and gloves, ignoring the others and steering.

More and more strange cyclists crowded the road. There was a family in a four-wheeled pedal car eating lunch as they rode. The parents sat side by side on a bench and pedalled while two babies in helmets and goggles sat on the floor in front of them banging their spoons and drooling on their bibs. Everywhere Frankie turned she saw another crazy bicycle. There were even people madly pumping strange flatbed cars that sped down the rail tracks that ran beside the road.

The road ended at a huge meadow. Mary and Frankie parked their bikes in a massive bike parking lot at one end. All over the meadow were coloured flags and tents. From the far end of the field came the sound of a crowd cheering and laughing. Frankie and Mary approached and peered through an opening in a set of high bleachers curved in a circle. Through the opening they could see actors in harlequin suits performing breathtaking maneuvers on unicycles. A man holding a pole balanced sparkling children at either end of it while he cycled atop a tall seat ten feet in the air. Mary looked at Frankie with laughing eyes and an impish smile. "What do you think, young Francesca?"

Frankie couldn't answer, she was so excited and happy.

It was a wonderful show. Mary bought them hotdogs and drinks. Then the actors wheeled out a long metallic tube made of honeycomb panels, each shining and translucent like mother of pearl. A small actor with a huge voice and a tall hat stood in the middle of the arena and shouted, "Can I have a volunteer from the audience to ride in our magnificent human-powered machine?" Frankie looked at Mary, who shrugged happily and said, "Why not?"

Frankie shot up her hand.

"You! Little girl with the fiery hair."

Frankie ran down with Dan hot on her heels. "Are dogs allowed?"

"Allowed? Dogs are *de rigeur*!"

"And one more!" cried the actor. "Let's get a boy. You." Frankie was brimming with excitement as a small boy half her age scampered down.

"And your name is?" asked the Master of Ceremonies.

"Bingo Sharmsky!" squeaked the boy, puffing out his chest proudly.

"Alright, Bingo and Frankie. Right this way." They marched after the actors, Bingo squirming and skipping, squeaking and clapping his tiny hands, and filed into a little door cut into the curved end of the tube. The actors wore sleek, silver suits and their faces were painted with blue-and-white diamond checks. Their lips were beautiful curving rosebuds and on their prancing feet were silver boots as thin as ballet slippers. Inside the tube was a pair of pedal seats on either side of a central aisle. The mother-of-pearl panels that made up the walls of the tube were transparent from the inside. Silent and smiling, the actors ushered Frankie up to the front of the vehicle, where it opened into a wide reclining seat. As she sat down, the ceiling over her head slid away. She and Bingo and Dan settled on the seat and an actor pulled a long seatbelt across all three of them. Behind the seat, two actors settled onto their stationary bicycles and the rest of the actors pantomimed a salute and farewell, then marched out like toy soldiers, smiles on their rosebud lips. A gong as deep and ringing as the sounding of a whale reverberated in the very walls of the machine.

The cyclists leaned forward and started to pedal — *whir, whir, whir.* Frankie felt as if the craft was tensing to launch. Huge pterodactyl wings unfolded from the sides of the tube and swept down once, twice, pulling the vehicle up each time with a gentle bobbing lift, so that smoothly, slowly, with each successive stroke of the massive yet delicate wings, the tube rose above the bleachers and the startled crowd below.

Holding her breath, Frankie saw that beyond the fair, the ground dropped away to a sweeping valley of tiny roads and farms, cars and trees. All around her the sky was filling with floating constructions that were more air than the material they were made of. Everything was brushed with the indistinct, pale magical blue of dusk. The distant horizon softly merged with the sky, and overhead early stars winked. Looking down, Frankie saw lozenges of gold light from suppertime kitchen windows and travelling headbeams from the toy cars of the miniature world below. Bingo was beside himself with excitement. He squirmed free of the seatbelt and leaned out so far he almost fell off into space. With reflexes that surprised both of them, Frankie shot out her arm and yanked him back. She pulled him onto her lap and wrapped her arms firmly around him.

"Just watch," she whispered into his ear. "Isn't it amazing?"

"Yes," he whispered and leaned back against her. They were held together in a state of wonderment as the strange mechanical bird slowly floated through the evening sky.

Chapter Nineteen

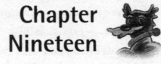

The next morning, Mary rode partway to the hotel with Frankie. Before she turned back, she outlined the plan that Frankie was to follow.

"I can't come all the way to the hotel with you because Maurice Ravel is still in intensive care. But you remember that little boy you went up in the air with? Well, his mother and I got to talking and I found out they are going to be staying at the hotel too. They're going for a family reunion. She said she'd keep an eye out for you, although she had an awful lot of children and seemed just a little distracted. I hope she remembers. Anyway, I've booked a room for you to stay in tonight. It's on my credit card. And you've got the money Augusta gave you to buy meals. Let me see it."

Frankie took off her knapsack and showed Mary her money.

"Good, good. That should be plenty. Remember, you can charge things to the room if you have to. I told them you were my niece and that I've been unavoidably delayed. Call me tomorrow. With any luck, Maurice Ravel will be out of danger by then and you'll have found the ring. We'll arrange to meet so I can come and take you to Professor Proteus' house. I don't want to actually step onto hotel property and run the risk of Zelda recognizing me. In any case, phone me to let me know how you're making out. Don't forget."

Frankie kept nodding seriously, listening hard and saying, "Yes Mary, thank you Mary."

Mary laughed. "Now, just carry on down this road until you come to the lake. Turn off onto the trail that runs along the lake shore and it will take you to the hotel. Take care. I know Dan and the Hippogriff will watch out for you, but take care all the same." And she kissed Frankie on the forehead, put her hand on her cheek and smiled into her eyes. "I know we're going to be lifelong friends."

By midday, Frankie came to the turnoff. It was just as Mary had described it. Dan barked and pointed the way with his nose. The road wound down until they were beside a lake where a sandy path ran under a row of pine trees beside the water. Sunlight streaming through the branches flickered over them as they rode and sparkled blindingly on breeze-fed waves. The air was soft and warm and the tires whispered over sand and pine needles.

The path rose higher and higher above the water until they came to the edge of a sandy bluff. Below was a beach crowded with sunbathers: Children with buckets and shovels, and women in bikinis with their straps down and skin glistening with sunscreen, bronzed men with sleek muscles, and pale men with stick legs and hairy stomachs. A lifeguard on a high chair posed like a movie star in her sunglasses, forgetting about the white goop on her peeling nose. Another lifeguard in a rowboat with a whistle and a megaphone rowed with one arm in agitated circles, blowing his whistle and shouting through the funnel, "YOU! Stop that! And you! Stop that too! That is definitely NOT ALLOWED!" And he hauled a squiggling fat child in orange water wings into the boat, clamping one foot down on the squirming striped bathing suit and flopping flippers. He turned red-faced with outrage. "That's it. You're all in breach of the rules. Everyone out of the water!" But no one paid any attention to him and the guppy in water wings slid out from under his foot and flopped over the side, squirming away as happy as a seal.

Beyond the beach rose the spires and turrets of the hotel. Pennant flags blew from the turrets and striped blue awnings presided over outdoor lunchers sitting at curlicued cast-iron tables and chairs. Pristine tablecloths fluttered like magnolia petals in the beachside breeze and a pianist tinkled out song stylings.

Frankie felt all the pent-up tension of the trip flow out of her. She breathed a sigh of pure pleasure. "What a place, Dan. I've never seen anything so beautiful," she whispered as they coasted lazily down to the hotel, following the sandy dappled path. They wound past the stables, from which emanated clipclopping, snorting, and rich horsey smells. Then a quaint green sign with cursive script directed them to the tennis courts, the band-shell and the bicycle shed. Frankie hopped down. She wheeled Hippogriff into a warm shed striped with dusty shafts of sunlight, and parked in a bike stand alongside many other bikes. Taking the plaid blanket out of the basket, she called, "Come on Dan, it's bathtime!"

They pattered down a dusty path through the trees towards the sounds of the beach. Stopping at the edge of the sand, Frankie took off her sneakers and felt the soft shock of hot sand under her feet. She and Dan walked through the heat and shouting and coconut smells of suntan oil. Finding an empty space in the midst of the sunbathers, Frankie dropped her pack and the blanket and stripped down to her bathing suit as fast as she could. She stepped out of her overalls and yanked off her T-shirt, not noticing that the green string with her ring came flying off with it. She ran for the water, Dan overtaking her and bounding ahead until, with a great leap and a delighted squeal, they both splashdived into the lake.

They paddled, floated and played forever in the delicious cool water. Then, clean as new pennies, they flopped down onto the blanket to dry in the sun. "This is the life, eh, Dan?"

When Frankie had thrown off her T-shirt, her ring flew through the air and landed on the towel of a bored teenaged girl lying on the beach reading a romance novel. The girl sighed and dropped the book, longing for love and someone cute to suddenly appear in her life. She turned over and hit her nose on a ring.

"That wasn't there before." The girl sat up and studied the ring. She looked around for the handsome but shy boy who must have tiptoed up and left it there. It must be someone she'd managed to overlook, even though she'd been hungrily scanning the resort guests, desperate to find *someone* to fall in love with. In romance novels, lakeside resorts were ideal locations for summer love. She undid the knot in the string and tossed the green strand on the sand, then slid the ring onto her wedding finger. She was gazing at her hand, admiring how elegant it looked, when a shadow fell over her. She looked up into the blinding sun at a tall dark figure. Her heart pounded with eagerness.

"Where'd you get that?" The voice of her mother came out of the shadowy figure.

"Oh God!" The girl flopped down, throwing her hand over eyes, wretched with disappointment.

"Well? I'm speaking to you, Annabelle Sharmsky!"

"It was just here," Annabelle sulked.

"Well, someone's lost it. Take it off and turn it in at the front desk at once!"

Annabelle groaned, then suddenly remembered the cute guy at the desk — well, not ugly, at least. His nametag said "Justin." She got to her feet and hurried in to the front desk as languidly as possible.

"Can I help you, miss?" asked the youth behind the desk.

"Hello, Justin," Annabelle said throatily, flipping her ponytail. "My name is Annabelle." Justin blushed deeply, accentuating his imperfect complexion. Annabelle slid her brown hand across the counter and wiggled her fingers at him. "I found this on the beach. Any idea who it belongs to?"

Justin's eyes bulged. Every person on staff had been told of the reward of $250 that would be given to any person who found a ring in the lake — a gold ring like this one, with a pink cameo and blue sapphires. There was an artist's rendering of it on the bulletin board in the staff room. Everyone knew that the hotel owner had even had the lake dredged looking for it. This version looked very tarnished and scratched, but it definitely fit the description.

The desk clerk leapt for the phone and hit the red button. "Ms. Halberton-Ffrench? There's something down here I think you should see." He listened for a moment then cupped his hand over the receiver and whispered, "It's the ring."

⌣•

Zelda Halberton-Ffrench whispered "Mommy" and took the ring in trembling fingers up to her luxurious suite in the penthouse. She sank down onto her curved cream-coloured leather sofa. She took of her glasses and pressed a trembling hand across her eyes. Then, taking a deep breath, she looked down and opened her hand. The ring didn't look as nice as she'd remembered. Rather tatty, really. She tried to put it on. She was a big woman and could only get the ring onto the tip of her baby finger.

Nothing happened. Nothing at all. The magic must have drained away after nearly sixty years at the bottom of the lake.

Zelda remembered the night before her father's funeral, how she had hid behind the coffin, and how her maddeningly self-righteous baby sister's adoration had quickly turned to accusation. Deeply disappointed, she locked the ring away in her jewelry box.

~.

Frankie and Dan joined a group of children digging an enormous moat around a sandcastle. When that was completed they dug mightily to create a long channel to the lake. When they were halfway to the lake Frankie decided to branch off to dig a tributary, thinking it would be even more exciting to see the water rush up two arms to the moat. The sun was in her eyes, a light breeze tickled the water into tiny wavelets. Everything sparkled. Flecks of silica and mica in the shifting sand made it look like it was made of diamonds and gold. Dan rushed up and down, stopping every now and then to dig madly like the terrier he was. All around Frankie were happy children's voices. One little girl had the sweetest laugh. It was so happy, tinkling and pretty — almost like stars or bells. Frankie looked around but couldn't figure out which child owned that laugh. She dug her own channel with the glittering light in her eyes and laughter in her ears. Dan ran up and down excitedly until the channel reached the water. Frankie clapped delightedly as the water came rushing in to fill the moat. Then she sat leaning contentedly on one hand, picking up fistfuls of sand with the other and letting it run out through her fingers. The tinkling laughter was even clearer now, and it slowly dawned on her that all the children were a ways away, starting a new fortification. Strange, thought Frankie.

The afternoon lengthened and shadows leapt and danced on the sand. Mothers called their children out of the sun for supper and the crowd thinned to a few stragglers. Frankie's stomach started to rumble. She and Dan got up and wandered into the vast ringing lobby of the hotel. Frankie hopscotched on the black-and-white marble tiles and leaned backward to stare at the sparkling chandelier. How did something that big stay hanging up there?

The imposing figure of Hotelier Zelda Halberton-Ffrench strode across the marble foyer. She frowned at the wild-haired little girl and her dog. She would have reprimanded them with her usual, "Where are your minders? This is a hotel lobby, not a playground!" but this evening she was lost in her own disappointed thoughts. She strode on without a word.

Unaware that Zelda had just passed behind her, Frankie stopped to read a signboard. It had movable white letters that declared:

WELCOME TO THE SHARMSKY SHOWBIZ
FAMILY REUNION — BANQUET ROOM #3.
Absolutely no juggling under any circumstances.

"Hey Dan, those are the people Mary talked to." As she said this, Frankie noticed that the little kids who ran up and down one of the corridors leading off the lobby kept popping in and out of a pair of double doors halfway down the hall. Lots of them were dressed up, but some wore only shorts and T-shirts. She could hear the clink of cutlery and a gallumphing orchestra playing "What's New, Pussycat?" The smell of hotel cooking wafted through the doors. A small boy with a minute pink mouth bent into an impish "v" ran up and smacked Frankie on her bare leg. Frankie looked down. "Bingo!" It was the little boy who'd gone up in the air with her at the Human-Powered Vehicle Fair. He grinned up at her, then squatted down and patted Dan, who licked his face and barked. Bingo toppled backwards onto his behind in surprise.

"Come on!" shouted a bigger boy from the doorway

"Come on," invited Bingo, then scampered off. Frankie and Dan looked at each other, then scampered right after him, through the double doors and into Banquet Room #3.

Hundreds of Sharmskys milled in the wide banquet hall. They ate at large tables, laughing and standing up to propose toasts. They propelled each other up and down the dance floor and shouted and waved at each other across the room and pointed excitedly at nametags.

"I'm Doris' little girl," an old lady with a blue rinse shouted down at an even more elderly man in an electric wheelchair.

Frankie looked around, wondering where to go next. Then she spotted a group of four large round tables together in one corner of the room. The tables were full of children. She ran over and quickly slid into a chair and immediately had a plate of bitty pizza, a bitty burger and three bitty chicken nuggets placed in front of her by the waitress. She drank three glasses of pink fruit punch from one of the jugs on the table and passed down a burger to Dan, followed by the somewhat mauled remains of another dinner abandoned by the five-year-old next to her. None of the kids cared if she was Ginny's girl or Freddy's cousin. At one point, a man with a big smile and a very pink face swung up and bellowed, "Everything hocus pocus, ankle-biters?"

"Yes," they all chorused. So, rejoicing, he sailed off again, listing gently to the side as he waved genially and hallooed to one and all.

People sang funny songs at the piano or told jokes. Then a band got up to play. "Are there any children in the audience who would like to come up and join us for the annual Sharmsky Jam?" Frankie couldn't have said what came over her, but she pulled her penny whistle out of her knapsack and ran up with the other children. The singer took the microphone around and got each child to introduce themselves. When he got to Frankie he looked delighted. "Well, what do we have here? A leprechaun with a tin whistle. Will you bewitch us with a tune?"

Frankie was giddy with excitement. A jam! Just like with Dad! "I'll try."

"What'll you play for us, then?"

"I don't know yet," she said, putting the mouthpiece to her lips. Out came a lively tune. It just popped into her head. The other musicians smiled and nodded to each other, the leader shouted, "One two three four," and the fiddles, guitar, mandolin and drums all joined in. It turned into a mad jig and everyone in the audience cheered. They clapped in time and rushed to the dance floor.

When the tune finally came to an end everyone wanted to know its name. The band leader turned to Frankie.

"I don't know," she said. "It just came into my head."

"Well, that's pretty impressive. I say we call it Frankie's Reel and let's play it again!" When the band finally took a break, Frankie collapsed into a chair and guzzled a glass of pink lemonade. A man with tufts of grey hair, thick glasses, a purple nose and a nametag that read "The Great Roscoe Sharmsky, Iowa" came up to her.

"What's your name again, kid?" He cupped his hand to his ear and leaned forward.

"Frankie."

"Frank! Frank, you say. Whoever heard of calling a girl Frank? Your parents got gender issues?"

"Francesca."

"Francesca! Why didn't you say so? Anyways, you ever need a job kid, here's my card."

The card said: "Roscoe Sharmsky (The Great). Master of Clowning, Impressario Extraordinaire."

The band took a break, but not the dancers. Old-time recorded music came on and Frankie did the twist and the Chicken Dance with the other kids. They played tag, threading excitedly through the press of adults bopping on the dance floor or grouped around tables on chairs tied with gently bobbing balloons. And somehow, at the close of the night, she ended up like so many of the other children, curled up asleep under a table like a fairy under a toadstool.

Chapter
Twenty

Frankie woke up in a giant double bed. She stretched under the lovely sheets and wiggled her toes, feeling extremely comfy. Dan walked up from where he was sleeping at the foot of the bed and licked her nose.

"What a fantastic party, Dan! If only Dad could have been there." She remembered being woken up by Bingo's mother, Angel, who'd already collected her knapsack. Frankie had fallen asleep again on the flowered chintz sofa in the lobby while Bingo's mother got Frankie's room key for her. The busy clerk then turned back to the tipsy questions and requests of a small mob of Sharmskys. Angel picked up the heavy unconscious Bingo, who was curled up like a puppy beside Frankie, and nudged Frankie awake. They all went up in the elevator. In the hallway Angel silently handed Bingo to another adult and walked Frankie to her room, tucked her in and told her to come down tomorrow morning to the dining room — "But don't bring Dan into the restaurant" — for breakfast at the children's table.

"Night, Angel."

"Sleep tight, Frankie."

Now, at the thought of breakfast, Frankie leapt out of bed and ran to the bathroom ("My own bathroom — wow!") to wash her face and brush her teeth. "Sorry Dan," she called as she closed the door to her room, "you'll have to stay here until after breakfast."

Bingo waved to her as she walked into the dining room, so she went and sat with him and his brother and six or seven other kids. The waitress brought her a plate of waffles, assuming she was another of the numberless Sharmskys. None of the Sharmskys ever stopped talking and kids came and went from the table non-stop. When Frankie was finished eating, she smuggled out a napkin full of waffles for Dan.

It was still very early but Frankie and Dan headed out to the beach again. Frankie stopped at the edge of the sand for Dan to pee on a few trees and chase squirrels. Her mind returned to the tinkling laughter she'd heard the day before, the oddness of it. Dan came back grinning all over himself, so she headed out across the beach, past the moat and the castle, over to where she'd sat yesterday. She stood and closed her eyes. The breeze ruffled her hair. The sun sparkled, making her closed eyelids glow red and gold. Had she imagined the giggling? She moved towards the pier. And there it was, very faint. On the pier, it got louder. She walked down the wooden planks to the end and then back, then to one side, then the other. The laughter was clearest at the very end on the side facing the hotel. She looked over the side. The water was deep there, but clear. She could see the ridged sand on the bottom and tiny sand-coloured fish flicking back and forth. There was a big grey rock half-imbedded in the sand. The laughter seemed to be coming from the rock itself.

To get her Seal Badge, Frankie had had to jump into the deep end and swim back to the side, tread water for thirty seconds and dive three feet to pick up a rubber ring. She peered into the water again. This was way over her head. The red letters on the wooden pier said six feet, and at the end where the diving board was, it said fifteen feet. There was a ladder that went into the water so you could climb back up after diving off.

Frankie jumped in. The water fizzed with bubbles and she bounced up to the surface. She flailed to the ladder, and clung to it gasping. Dan looked down at her.

"I barely went down at all. I'm going to have to dive," she told Dan. She climbed back up and stood on the side of the pier, shivering in the fresh morning air. She hadn't learned how to dive yet, so she did her best imitation. She leaned over, pointed her hands over her head and sort of dropped into the water headfirst. She only got halfway to the bottom before she panicked and zipped up to the surface.

The third time, she took a deep breath, bounced off her toes and dove with some spring behind her. In the water she pulled hard with long strokes, like her dream of flying except now she was fighting to go down through the light-shafted water. The pressure built in her head and the laughter was very clear as she touched the rock. Then she had to shoot back up to the surface for air. The fifth time she tried, she went straight down as fast as possible. She felt around the bottom of the rock for an edge, hoping to turn it over. She knew things were easier to lift under water. But the rock seemed to be like an iceberg, just the tip showing above the sand. No chance of turning it over. It was pyramid-shaped, sloping on three sides but straight down, rough and craggy, on the fourth. She could hear the giggling even more clearly now. It glittered inside her entire body. Then her finger encountered a hole on the straight side. Something wiggled, and a tiny fish shot out of the hole. She felt inside the hole again, hoping nothing would bite her. Her head and lungs were bursting. When she got to the surface, she was gasping. She clawed the few metres to the ladder. Hanging on, she opened her hand. The ring: glittering and beautiful, as if freshly polished; the gently smiling woman's face in the cameo and the sapphires as blue as the bluest eye. The ring had called to her. Maybe it sang to Augusta, but for her it giggled. Frankie smiled.

"Oooh, that's pretty, Frankie."

Frankie looked up to see little Bingo Sharmsky peering over the edge of the pier at her. She climbed up the ladder.

"Can I see it? What is it?"

"It's a ring, Bingo. Don't tell anyone, okay?"

"Okay, I won't tell."

She opened her hand and Bingo snatched the ring, racing off and shrieking at the top of his lungs, "I've got a ring! I've got Frankie's ring!"

He was incredibly fast and Frankie was exhausted. She couldn't catch up, but Dan raced beside Bingo as if this was the best fun he'd ever had. Bingo ran in through the french doors of the hotel, through the restaurant and into the lobby. Frankie finally leapt on him, tackling him to the carpet in the sitting area where Roscoe was asleep in a large armchair.

"Wha? Wha?" gabbled Roscoe, waking up.

Bingo was curled into a tight, shrieking, giggling ball. "A beautiful ring. I've got a beautiful ring!"

"Shh, shh, Bingo. Give it to me. It belongs to Augusta," Frankie whispered hoarsely. She couldn't pry it off him. He was shut up tighter than a clam.

Suddenly, a big hand clamped onto Frankie's arm. She was whipped to her feet like a toy, then another hand grasped the top of her head like a grapefruit. The fingers squeezed and tilted her head back. Her eyes travelled up past an extremely large bosom to a nametag that read "Zelda Halberton-Ffrench, Chief Executive Officer and Owner, Hotel Magnificat." Then her head was violently swivelled towards the much smaller personage of Roscoe Sharmsky, who was sitting with his hands clamped onto the armrests and a look of astonished horror on his face.

"Do you know this child?" demanded Zelda.

The Great Roscoe's little head was throbbing. He'd had too much punch the night before at the party, become a tad frisky, and ... well, some juggling had taken place. There'd been an accident and people weren't too happy with him. His wife wouldn't let him into their hotel room. ("This is absolutely the last time you humiliate me in public, Roscoe Sharmsky!") So he'd fallen asleep in the large armchair in the lobby. "Sure," he said slowly, "she played the penny whistle last night."

"Yes, yes, but is she a Sharmsky?" barked the hotel manager impatiently.

"Well, if she isn't, she should be. A born ham if ever I saw one."

Zelda didn't like this answer. She looked like she was ready to slap someone. "Is she a Sharmsky or not?" she bellowed.

"She might not be a Sharmsky ... but then again, she might be. There's too many of us to know for sure," Roscoe stammered.

Estelle Sharmsky, Roscoe's wife, bustled up in slippers and a flowered robe. "What have you done now, Roscoe?" Roscoe made shushing gestures and pointed with his thumb at Frankie, raising and wiggling his eyebrows. He made a throat-cutting motion with his hand.

Estelle, who really had a tender heart, took it all in. A worried look crossed her face.

But Zelda wasn't paying attention to Roscoe anymore. Her fingers tilted Frankie's head back around. Her beet-red face loomed in towards Frankie's. "*Who* are *you*?"

"Frankie Rudderless."

"And *what* is *that*?"

"Dan the dog."

"That sounds vaguely familiar, like a nightmare I might have had." Zelda turned to Bingo. "You! Horrible small boy. Open your hand."

Bingo did as he was told, and Zelda snatched at the ring in his palm. "WHERE did you get that?" she screeched.

Bingo, for once, was mute. He stuck his thumb in his

mouth and pointed at Frankie. Zelda turned on her. "How did you get into my room? You're a thief!"

"I am not!" responded Frankie indignantly.

"Young lady — if that's what you are — I know very well that you have stolen this ring because it is mine. We'll see what the police have to say about this."

"Actually," interrupted Roscoe. "This girl is practically ours. We're putting her in the show." He whispered to Estelle behind his hand, "With hair like that, she won't need any stage makeup."

"Out of my way, clown!" ordered Zelda as she strong-armed Frankie past the Sharmskys. Frankie's feet barely touched the floor all the way to the owner's office.

"Detention without due process," hollered Roscoe. "That does it! I'm calling a press conference." He turned to Estelle. "And what publicity!"

"Roscoe! Shame on you!"

"What shame? Two birds with one stone is all —"

"You are positive this is your ring, ma'am?" asked the plainclothes police officer.

"I know my ring, detective." Zelda opened the office door and bellowed down the marble hall to the desk clerk, "Justin, go up to my suite and bring down my jewelry box." Justin scurried up like a mouse in glasses and took the proffered keys. He returned in minutes, staggering under the weight of a mahogany box large enough to bury a junior typist in.

"I think you will find that my box, which is always kept locked, has been forced," Zelda announced smugly.

Then, to Justin, "Well, show him! Show him the lock."

Justin fumbled the box onto the desk and slid it around. It was still locked.

"Hmmm ... Well, she must be a lock-picker." Zelda glared at Frankie and Dan. "They're very likely members of a gang of international jewel thieves. Thieves train children and animals, you know. To get into small spaces. No one ever suspects them." She looked at Justin. "Well, open it! Open it! Not that key, idiot boy! Oh! Do I always have to do everything myself?" She opened the box and gasped. The police officer and Justin leaned in. A ring just like the one she'd taken from Bingo gleamed inside the box.

"This is more cunning than I suspected. My ring has been replaced by a perfect replica!" Perplexed, Zelda picked up the ring in the jewel box, replaced it with its double, looked at the new ring, then picked up the first.

The detective leaned in even closer to examine the rings. He glanced at Frankie, then shielding his mouth with his hand, whispered to Zelda, "You may have a point there, ma'am."

"Of course I have a point!" Zelda boomed. "Do you doubt my word, officer?"

"Not at all!" the detective spluttered, reddening. "I *mean*," he whispered, "about there being a ring of juvenile thieves."

Zelda peered around the police officer to look at Frankie, narrowing her eyes suspiciously. She lowered her voice. "Go on."

"Unbeknownst to the general Joe Q. Public, and strictly *entre nous*, a criminal who goes by the alias of

The Crocodile has just been released in the vicinity. He is known for kidnapping children and brainwashing them to steal for him. By the looks of it," he jerked his head at Frankie and nodded knowingly, "he may be up to his old tricks again."

"I see," whispered Zelda.

The police officer whirled around and shouted down at Frankie, "Who are you working for, Franklin?"

Before Frankie could reply, Dan leapt up with a growl and bit the police officer's tie.

"Get him off! Get him off!" squealed the detective as he spun in circles. Dan hung on tight. Zelda stumbled backwards and took shelter behind her desk, like a true executive.

Frankie could now see both rings sitting in the box. She leapt forward, grabbed the ring she'd retrieved from the lake, and ran from the room and across the echoing lobby, pelting as hard as her legs would go towards the massive front doors.

From behind her desk, Zelda ignored the whirling dervish in front of her, leaned forward and peered into the box. She narrowed her eyes at the remaining ring. Then she lifted the bifocals resting on her capacious bosom and looked again. "It's a fake!" she gasped. "This is a fake! She's taken the real one!" She reached across her desk and swatted the police officer with that morning's *Financial Post*. "YOU! Public servant! Stop tap dancing with that dog and GET MY RING!"

As Frankie darted across the hotel lobby, a room service trolley came rolling out from behind a pillar. Frankie crashed smack into it and went sprawling. A moment later, Dan ran up and licked her nose. She sat up, clutching Dan around the neck as the police officer, Zelda and Justin descended on her. They all reached for her at once, bashing heads and getting in each other's way.

"Get out of my way! I am the owner of this hotel," commanded Zelda. She pried open Frankie's fists. No ring. She grabbed Frankie's knapsack and emptied it onto the floor. She kicked at Frankie's stuff, then whirled on the girl, her eyes bulging and her nostrils flaring,

"Where. Is. It? Horrible child!"

Frankie shook her head, backing away, her lips pressed firmly together. Zelda lunged at her.

"Ma'am, I really must insist we wait for a female officer before we search the girl any further," protested the detective.

Zelda whirled around. Her pupils were dilated and her eyes bloodshot. "Where's that ugly little dog?" But Dan was nowhere to be seen. "Well, lock her up until the female officer comes, then. And I want everyone looking for that dog." She glared at Justin. "Move!"

～·

"That Zelda is just as scary as Augusta said," thought Frankie. She was sitting in the laundry room in the basement. There was a small barred window near the ceiling but at least it smelled clean. The door opened just long enough for her knapsack to be flung in, then slammed shut again. She heard the detective explaining that he had to call a female officer and a social worker to interview her. Then they would take her to a temporary foster home for wayward children until they could contact her parents.

By and by, lunch was brought in by spotty Justin, who stuttered an apology for the uncomfortable accommodation.

"Looks like you're going to be here for a while. The social worker in the village is in the middle of a crisis and can't come until tomorrow." He put down the tray. "What's it like being an international jewel thief?" he asked admiringly.

"I'm not an international jewel thief."

"You're not?" Justin looked disappointed.

There was a knock on the door.

"Who is it?" asked Justin.

"It's me, Annabelle."

Justin scrambled to his feet and ran to the door. "What do you want?"

"You're wanted upstairs."

Justin opened the door. He was blushing. "How come they sent *you*? You're not an employee."

"I just made that up. I wanted to see you."

"Why?"

"Because I want you to take me in your strong, manly arms and kiss me."

"You do?" Justin's voice squeaked in a most unmanly way. Frankie couldn't believe it. What a disgusting thing to say right in front of her. Couldn't Annabelle have found a better place to waylay Justin? She had him backed into a corner of the room, up against the dryer.

"I'm going to kiss you now, Justin. Kiss you like you've

never been kissed before," said Annabelle, getting ready to pounce. Justin's eyes were closed. His lips were sort of pouting out. It was difficult to say whether he looked eager or terrified. Frankie noticed Annabelle's hand was wiggling behind her back.

"You are my soulmate and passion is throbbing in my breast." Annabelle clearly found it easy to reel off romance-novel dialogue.

"That's a strange thing to do when you're about to kiss someone," thought Frankie, staring at Annabelle's waving hand. She wrinkled her nose. Annabelle's hand was really flapping now — and pointing. Pointing? *To the open door*!

As Frankie flew through the doorway, she heard Annabelle moan, "Surrender to my embrace, my prince!"

Frankie crouched at the top of the stairs, then snuck down the carpeted hallway. She hovered at the edge of the vast lobby, then crept forward, past Zelda's office. She could hear Zelda arguing with the police detective. Frankie was halfway to the entrance when she was stopped in her tracks.

"Frankie! We've been looking everywhere for you," rang out the penetrating cry of Bingo Sharmsky.

Roscoe popped up from behind a newspaper in one of the lobby armchairs. "Shush, Bingo!"

But it was too late. Zelda and the detective came running out the office. Roscoe gestured at Frankie. "Amscray, kid. I'll divert them." He grabbed the tea things from the table and starting juggling, walking straight into the path of Zelda and the law.

Frankie streaked off and through the immense gothic-arched doors of the hotel. Hair flying, she bounded down the wide steps and raced around the corner, past the green sign with the curving arrow, to the bicycle shed. As she heaved the bike from the rack, Dan's head popped up from Hippogriff's basket.

"There you are, Dan!" She could hear a lot of shouting and the sound of running feet getting closer. She stepped astride the bike and put a foot on the pedal. Then she gripped the handles, lowered her head and prayed, "Hippogriff, don't fail me now!"

The bike shot out through the open door like a guided missile. Frankie's red hair streamed raggedly behind her like the flame of a roaring jet engine. The detective gasped in terror and leapt off the path. Frankie's feet on the pedals were a blur as they zoomed past Zelda. Justin trailed behind, panting, clutching the giant jewelry box. Bingo and Roscoe stood on the hotel steps waving, and as Frankie and Dan swooped down the curving drive and away down the road they shouted after her, "See you at the next reunion!"

"We're fugitives from the law now, Dan," said Frankie. As she pedalled, she reached down to Dan's neck. She felt in his thick fur along his collar until she came to his dog tag, and there, hanging alongside it, Augusta's ring.

On the cool black-and-white marble floor of the lobby of the Hotel Magnificat, nestled beside a potted palm, lay a sepia-toned photograph that had fallen out of Frankie's knapsack. It was of two little girls wearing old-fashioned bathing suits and squinting into the sunshine as they sat in a rowboat on a pretty lake. Zelda bent to pick it up. She straightened up slowly, wonderingly.

"Augusta!"

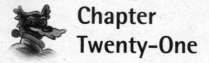# Chapter
Twenty-One

Ron hurried home from a round of appointments, support group and shopping. The social worker Marisa was due any minute to see how he was doing. He had just finished putting the groceries away when he heard the tinkle of his old wind-up door chime. He swung open the door and proudly ushered in Marisa. He made a grand sweep of his hand at the clean house. He and Violet had laboured for hours and hours.

"Eh? Eh? *Inspeckable* or what?" Ron used Violet's word.

Marisa was impressed. She'd taken a little sniff as she stepped past Ron on the way in. No liquor smell. The house was indeed inspeckable. She felt genuinely happy. "It's wonderful, Ron. You've done so much in such a short time."

"Well, I've had help actually. The lady next door lent me her housekeeper." Ron led Marisa to the interplanetary turquoise kitchen table and put a cup of tea in front of her. "I've got so much to tell you."

"Where's Francesca?"

"She's at tennis camp."

Marisa looked startled.

"It's a long story," explained Ron. "Anyway, it's —"

The phone rang. Ron picked it up. "Hello there, Augusta," he said cheerily. Marisa watched Ron turn white. His mouth opened but no words came out. Still listening to the voice in the receiver, he turned to Marisa with bewilderment and fear in his eyes.

Alarmed, Marisa asked, "What is it, Ron?"

He put the phone down. "Frankie's missing."

A few long minutes later, Ron and Marisa sat in Augusta's kitchen, listening to her tell the real story of where Frankie was.

"Why didn't you tell me, Violet?" Ron turned to the housekeeper accusingly.

Violet twisted her apron. She was on the verge of tears. "She made me promise not to." Violet glared at her employer. "*She* said it was the only way to keep Francesca out of the foster home."

"I wasn't going to put her into a foster home!" protested Marisa. "I was giving Ron the chance to make some changes before making my recommendations."

"Everyone listen to me!" Augusta shouted. "What matters now is finding Francesca. She was supposed to call my friend Mary from the hotel but Mary phoned me to say that she never did. The hotel said someone checked in under the name of Dr. Dahliwal but they couldn't tell Mary what that person looked like. The night clerk couldn't remember because it was so busy. The entire hotel was in some kind of uproar because of a huge family reunion and some sort of police investigation. I can't reach my other friend, Professor Proteus, who was supposed to take care of Francesca. He doesn't seem to have a phone."

"Why doesn't Mary go to the hotel and look for her?" Ron demanded.

"Because Maurice Ravel is dying!" Augusta wailed.

Ron was momentarily flummoxed. "But Maurice Ravel died ages ago."

"Not the composer, the skunk!"

Marisa couldn't stand it anymore. "Give me that phone," she demanded. "What's the name of the hotel and the closest town?" Everyone listened as Marisa took charge. She contacted the police station in Pigglestop and explained who she was. She carried on a three-way conversation and, with Augusta's help, relayed detailed descriptions of the missing girl, the bike and the dog.

"She'll be travelling by the Old Highway on the circle route," Augusta said. Marisa passed on that information and gave the police Augusta's number, Ron's number and her own cellphone number.

"They told me they only have a detective and two officers. One of them answered the phone, the other two are at the hotel investigating a spate of robberies. The officer assured me that a missing child takes priority and that they will be getting back to us immediately."

"I'm driving there now," Ron burst out.

"No, you're not." Marisa was firm. "You have no

license and will only make matters worse. And we don't know where she is. For all we know, she could be on her way home."

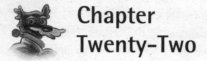

Chapter
Twenty-Two

The hot summer sun shone down on the black asphalt of the narrow country lane. Hippogriff, Frankie and Dan had ducked off the main road as soon as possible and had taken several twists and turns onto increasingly narrow roads. A boisterous river ran on one side of the road and trees on the other. The still air had a dusty, sweet smell. Frankie was hungry. She looked closer at the massed greenery at the side of the road and saw blueberry bushes heavy with ripe fruit. She hadn't had a chance to eat the lunch Justin had brought to her in the laundry room. She got off the bike and leaned it against a tree, then started picking fat juicy blueberries, popping them into her mouth in sweet bursting handfuls. Dan tried to eat them, but his sharp teeth couldn't cope with the little round berries and he just snapped the air comically, looking hopeful, then sad.

"Dan, what are we going to find for you to eat?" Frankie patted him apologetically with berry-stained fingers. Then she felt something squishy underfoot. She looked down.

"Ooo, yuck!" She lifted her foot off a giant squashed slug. Dan sniffed it, then *ate* it. "Oh gross!" Frankie laughed despite herself. Dan looked extremely pleased with himself and his tail resumed its jaunty dash as he hunted for another. Frankie began filling the front pocket of her knapsack with berries for later. Picking and eating, she and Dan wandered deeper and deeper into the forest, following a sunny green tunnel through the berry bushes.

Suddenly Dan started growling. At the same time, Frankie smelled an awful stink and heard a snuffling, muttering voice. All at once it became painfully clear why there was a tunnel through the blueberry bushes. Right in front of them, and filling up the tunnel entirely, was a very large brown bear.

Frankie froze, her fingers half-raised to her open purple-stained mouth. For a moment the bear seemed unsure of what to make of them, then came forward very fast and growling. Before she could stop him, Dan ran at the bear, barking furiously. The bear swiped at the little terrier with its long claws and hurled him through the air. Dan hit a fallen log and slid down into a clump of ferns. He didn't get up again. Frankie took a step backward, tripped over a root and fell sprawling. Her knapsack fell beside her, spilling blueberries and the jar of Bumble honey. With a pounding heart, she reached for the jar, unscrewed the lid and poured honey over the fallen berries, then rolled off the path and into the under-growth, the long ferns and grasses closing over her. She lay as still as possible.

A few heart-pounding moments later, she could hear the bear coming closer. Then she heard it sniffing and lapping up the honey-covered berries. She turned her head to peer through the grass. Now the bear was trying to lick out the inside of the jar. It seemed to have got its snout stuck. Honey oozed out and the bear went crazy, shaking its head to get the jar off. Growling and whimper-ing, wagging its head, licking dripping honey and pawing at the jar, it crashed off through the bushes. Frankie held her breath and listened to the sound of thrashing and snapping twigs and mutterings recede into the distance.

At last she blinked and found she was still breathing. Above her the sun still shone and green leaves fluttered against patches of blue sky. She heard the buzz of insects and the twitter of birds. Scrambling to her feet she bounded through the vegetation to the clump of ferns where Dan had landed. She knelt beside his small, still body. His eyes were closed. He seemed to be unconscious. There was no blood that she could see but he panted painfully. Tears welled in Frankie's eyes,

"Oh Dan, please don't die." She picked him up. He was warm and heavy. She buried her face in his fur. "My brave, brave friend. Don't die, Dan. Please." She stood up with him in her arms, staggered a little, then waded back through the bracken to the path. The distance back to the road seemed endless. How had they roamed so far from Hippogriff? Finally they came out at the road. But ... the bike was gone!

Frantically, Frankie looked up and down the road. She recognized the tree she'd leaned the bike against. It had a split from being hit by lightning. Then a sudden movement caught her eye. Across the narrow river on the other side of the road, a speeding figure flashed through the trees. On Hippogriff! She had to reach the other side. Carrying Dan in her arms she crossed the road and edged down the bank to the water's edge. She looked down into the clear, rushing water. On the bottom were big round smooth stones, pale green with algae. They seemed to go right across to the other bank.

I'll step from stone to stone, then it won't get too deep, she thought.

She waded in. The water was shockingly cold and fast. She stepped onto the first stone. It was as slick as wet soap. Before she could do anything, her feet were swept out from under her and she and Dan were pulled under. Frankie came up again, gasping and swallowing water, clutching Dan's collar in the frozen fingers of one hand, not knowing if he was underwater or not. On down the river they were swept and around a bend towards a small wooden footbridge. Frankie lunged to grab one of the pilings and pulled Dan around so she could see if he was alive or drowned. His brown eyes bulged and his little skull showed under the water-slicked fur. Despite his shivering he gave her nose a single grateful lick.

From timber to timber they inched towards shore, then floundered onto the bank. Kneeling and panting, Frankie grinned at the little dog,

"Dan, you're awake! Are you okay?" Frankie put her arms around him and kissed his wet fur. Her heart instantly felt lighter. "Come on, we've got to get Hippogriff back." She stood up. "Can you walk?"

Dan struggled to his feet and wagged his tail.

"Good boy!"

They crossed the bridge and followed the road through the trees on the other side of the river. At least the river had taken them quickly in the robber's direction. Up ahead through the trees, Frankie caught another glimpse of the thief. He was straining up a hill and the bike didn't seem to be making the hill any easier for him. She could see the thief getting off to push the bike. He stopped and kicked it.

"Hey!" Frankie shouted. "That's my bike!" But her voice came out too thin and weak to reach the thief. Frankie broke into a trot; maybe she could catch up. She turned to look at Dan. He was just sitting in the middle of the road, shrunken and mournful. Turning again, she caught a last glimpse of the thief jumping on her bike and disappearing from view somewhere up the hill.

"Dan, come on," she begged. "We can catch up to him, then we'll ride." Just how they were going to get the bike back from the thief when they did catch up with him was another matter. "I'll just have to think of *something*," Frankie thought firmly.

Despite her entreaties, Dan couldn't move. He tried to get up, then slumped down again. Frankie stood on the road feeling desperate to get going, then hurried back to Dan, taking off her pack as she went. She knelt down and tried to ease him into the knapsack. Dan was all legs and groans. She'd get one leg in and start on the other to find he'd pulled the first leg out. Or she'd get both legs in but got stuck on his tail. Finally he was all the way in, with his paws and face peeping out the top. She put her pack on back to front so she could carry Dan more easily, then resumed hurrying up the road. Her feet squelched in her wet runners. "You know, Dan," she mused, "I've never been out of the city before. Now here I am, on the run from the law, almost eaten by a bear, drowned in the river, and lugging an injured dog through the woods after a bike thief. Before, I would have run home crying. I was so scared of those bullies at school I bought them candy. But you know what, Dan? I don't feel scared, I'm mad. I want my bike back!"

Frankie followed the bike tracks through the woods and up the hillside, panting and leaning into the climb until they came to a wide wooden gate that blocked the road. Nailed to the gate was the skull of some horned animal. The gate was covered with signs that read: "No trespassing" and "Keep out. This means you."

"Well, too bad, too sad," said Frankie. Menace's slogan suited her determined mood. She lowered Dan through the rails and onto the ground, then squeezed through herself. On they went. The higher they climbed, the darker and denser the forest became until it suddenly opened up at the top of the hill. In the clearing was a high stone wall over which loomed the grey gables of an immense house surrounded by even taller trees. The bike tracks led them right up to a door in the wall. The door was solid wood except for a small barred opening near the top. Beside it, mounted on the wall, was a bronze plaque that read:

Dr. Curiman Proteus, Esq.
Professor of Metallurgy
1 River Road

Dr. Proteus! That sounded familiar. Frankie fumbled for Augusta's list of names and addresses. Augusta's words came back to her: *You must stay with Professor Proteus en route. He's been keeping some valuable papers for me. He seems to have forgotten to send them to me. He's a lovely, lovely man. Brilliant mind!*

"Oh no, Dan," exclaimed Frankie. "The thief has gone into Professor Proteus' house." She looked for a bell to ring or a way to get in. Then a voice from inside the wall cried, "Agh! Agh!" The voice, rough and high, sounded like a terrified old person. Professor Proteus? Frankie reached for the bars in the door and pulled herself up. Grunting with the effort, she peered through the opening. She could see Hippogriff lying on the cobblestones near the back door of the house with Dan's blanket spilling out of its basket.

"Agh!" came the voice again. Then it cried, "Haste makes waste!" Frankie's arms gave out and she slid down the door. She noticed a big iron key still in the lock. Maybe she could tiptoe in, grab the bike and ride for help. She turned the key. The gate swung open. She froze in the doorway, her eyes darting everywhere, but the courtyard appeared empty. Hunching her shoulders, she scurried forward and seized Hippogriff's handlebars. The door banged shut behind her. She whirled around to see the thief leaning against the door, swinging the key on his finger. He was a sneering young man with a lock of dark hair that flopped over his forehead.

"I don't think so," he jeered. "Put the bike down. It's mine."

Outraged, Frankie shouted, "It is not! You stole it from me!"

"Finders keepers," screeched the voice of the old man.

"Professor Proteus!" Frankie ran towards the voice, hoping for an ally. She ran through the open back door of the house and looked wildly around. The young man sauntered in after her.

"Professor Proteus," he whined, mimicking her horribly. "He's not here. In fact," he sniggered into his hand, "he's dead."

"Dead?" Frankie was horrified. "But I just heard him."

"Agh!" came the old man's voice again. Frankie turned quickly. What she'd assumed was old Professor Proteus was, in fact, a ragged parrot on a perch. "Never say die," the parrot cackled, shifting from foot to foot.

"Shut up or I'll boil you for supper!" cried the young man. He snatched a small gilded ceramic apple from the sideboard and hurled it at the bird. The parrot dodged neatly and the ornament shattered against the stone wall.

"Never make threats you can't carry out!" advised the parrot, but the thief ignored him and turned to Frankie.

"Now, just what is your business with the posthumous Professor Proteus?" he demanded. "I am Edgar Proteus Junior III and any of my foregone great-grandpapa's erstwhile business is now my business. And all this," he sniffed and waved his hand at the room, "is mine.

Including that bike that great-grandpapa built."

Edgar made a big bunny hop over to the wall and threw out his arm theatrically, pointing to a photograph hanging there.

Curious, Frankie went over and peered. The photo was old and showed a man in plaid riding britches beside a bicycle that looked very much like Hippogriff, down to the winged creature on the cap.

"See? See? Smarty pants!" Edgar crowed. And with a flourish he dropped the big skeleton key to the outer door into his shirt pocket. Smirking, he sauntered over to an armchair and flopped into it, throwing his leg over the arm. He stretched and yawned, patting his open mouth like an actor, and swung his leg back and forth.

Frankie watched this performance with increasing frustration. "But Professor Proteus gave the bike away. And the person he gave it to gave it to me. So tough luck, Edgar the Third!"

Edgar's leg stopped swinging. He frowned. "*Who* did he give it to?"

"Augusta Halberton-Ffrench, that's who," Frankie shot back.

"Uh oh," Edgar looked worried. He held his chin and mumbled to himself, "I seem to remember hearing about that."

"What? I can't hear you," taunted the parrot

Edgar leapt up and ran over to the perch, "Okay, okay Perry — I stole it! I'm sorry!" he yelled.

"Confession is good for the soul," Perry the parrot replied.

"Really! Well then ..." Edgar turned to Frankie. "It's your turn. What's your name and what are you doing here?"

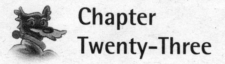

Chapter
Twenty-Three

Frankie stood defiantly, holding Dan, and faced Edgar Proteus III. "I'm Francesca Rudderless. Augusta sent me to find her ring."

"Did you find it?'

"Yes I did," she said proudly, "and it wasn't easy."

"Let's see," begged Edgar. Frankie parted Dan's fur to show the ring on his collar. Edgar's eyes widened with childish pleasure. "Good hiding place," he said admiringly.

"Thanks. We've been on the road for four days. We've been chased, locked up, almost eaten by a bear and then we had our bike stolen!"

"You did? Oh, you did." Edgar hung his head. "I said I was sorry."

"Didn't Augusta phone you to tell you I was coming to pick up some papers the professor left for her?"

Edgar looked suddenly embarrassed. He chewed his thumbnail and picked at the upholstery with his other hand. He hummed and stared at the ceiling as if there was something fascinating in the rafters.

"The phone's been cut off," he finally admitted.

Frankie knew all about things getting cut off. Ron had forgotten to pay the bills more than once. She sighed. She'd been hoping to phone Mary and Augusta. They must be worried about her, especially since she hadn't had time to phone Mary as planned. Outside the windows it was twilight and the room was becoming dim and cool. Frankie's shoes and clothes were still damp and she felt chilled. She wished she could warm up. Dan lay motionless on the floor beside her chair with his head between his paws.

"How about turning on the lights?" Frankie asked.

Edgar looked even more embarrassed.

"Don't tell me. You didn't pay the electricity bill either." Frankie sighed again.

"I'll light the lamp," Edgar offered and hopped up to get the kerosene lantern. While he was fiddling at the sideboard with the wick and the matches, Frankie asked him, "Don't you have any money to pay your bills?"

Edgar shook the match out and brought the lamp over to a low coffee table that sat on a faded Persian carpet in the middle of the room. "Oh, I've got bags of money," he said airily. "It's in the bank. When I want some I walk to the village and ask them to give me some. I'd take some money to the phone and electricity people but I don't know where they are." He went back to the sideboard and opened one of the doors. Unopened bills poured out and piled up on the floor. Some of them had FINAL NOTICE stamped on them in red ink.

"Oh, Edgar, why don't you write them a cheque?"

Edgar looked pained. He covered his face with his hands and moaned, "It just seemed so complicated. I don't know how. I thought if I ignored them they'd forget about me." He looked at Frankie through his fingers and said miserably, "I can't read."

Frankie was dumbfounded. "But you're a grown-up. Everybody can read!"

"Not everyone, showoff! Some of us have reasons." Edgar swung his leg onto the floor. He sat up primly with his hands on his knees. "I am a dyslexic insomniac," he announced.

"Oh, that's too bad," Frankie said sympathetically. "What does it mean?"

"Dyslexia means that my brain won't learn to read, and insomnia means I haven't slept in three years."

"Didn't Professor Proteus teach you how to read?" Frankie was appalled to think that someone with a brilliant mind wouldn't teach his own grandson how to read.

"Oh, he was busy with his inventions. I pretended everything was normal, pretended I'd read the books he gave me. I didn't want to disappoint him. How can you tell a genius you can't read? Anyway, he took care of everything and now that he's gone everything's fallen to pieces." Edgar gestured hopelessly at the bills and around the gloomy room.

Frankie suddenly felt sorry for Edgar. She concentrated for a moment, remembering when her mom was sick and the Menace was away. She used to bring her mom the mail and they opened it together. She remembered how Mom sent her to the bank with the bills to give to the teller to pay out of their account.

Frankie got up, went over to the pile of bills on the floor and started to sort through them. They were all from the same three companies, so she took one Final Notice from each and handed them to Edgar. "Okay Edgar, take these to the bank tomorrow and ask the teller to pay them out of your account."

"Really? The bank will do that?"

"Yup. Then hopefully, you'll get your phone and lights and heat back."

Edgar was delighted. "Amazing! You're so smart!"

"Not really. Everyone has to pay bills."

"Say, Francesca," Edgar asked, "are you hungry?"

"Starving."

"Goody. Let's go to the kitchen."

Edgar stood and picked up the lamp.

"Want some supper, Dan?" asked Frankie. Dan thumped his tail on the floor but didn't get up. "Oh well, upsy-daisy." Frankie picked him up. "Maybe you'll feel better after you eat."

Down the hall and up some stairs, down another hall and into a huge reception area, travelling through the house in an eccentric winding manner, one room opening into another, Edgar led the way like a tour guide: "Grand entrance hall ... games room ... library ... Oh, it's so fun to have company." He swung the lantern in a carefree way. The light and shadows slid crazily, revealing dusty unused furniture. Perry the Parrot flew after them, muttering to himself, making big winged shadows on the wall.

"Great-grandpapa's study. Everything kept just as he left it by his caring great-grandson."

Frankie looked around the lamp-lit room at the sagging, stuffed bookcases along every wall. The professor's desk was massive. But you could hardly see its green blotter the desk was so covered with gadgets and piles of papers spilling out of folders and organizer trays. There was also a globe, a brass banker's lamp with a green glass shade, and pens and pencils in a tarnished silver stein. The room had an assortment of strange lamps with bases of metal or pottery in the shapes of animals or people. Some of the lampshades were stained glass, some had dangling bobbles, others were made of some kind of yellowing translucent material stenciled with landscapes and scenes.

"How come he died?" Frankie asked, looking around the fascinating room.

Edgar shrugged. "He just did. I found him here. I thought he was having a snooze at his desk. He was always doing that. He was about a hundred years old, you know."

"Do you think the papers he left for Augusta might be in here?"

"I'm the last person to ask about that, Francesca. I don't know what any of this stuff is ... unless ..."

"Unless what?" Frankie prompted.

Edgar reached up to the top of a tall, narrow filing cabinet by the door. He brought down a wicker tray. "This is where he put stuff to be mailed." He held it out to Frankie. "Do you see anything in there?" Frankie put down Dan and took the tray to the desk. Edgar followed with the lamp.

"Well, it looks like Uncle Curious paid his bills." Frankie held up several envelopes.

"Uncle Curious," Edgar giggled. "That's a good name. Oh yes, the lights always came on when great-grandpapa was alive ... I wish he still was," he said wistfully.

Frankie was busy looking through the basket. "One for the Carolina Mechanical Toy Company and ... Ha!" Frankie held up a large envelope that was addressed to "Mrs. A. Halberton-Ffrench." "Good guess, Edgar!"

"Was it?" Edgar looked pleased.

Frankie put the letter into the bib pocket of her overalls and picked up Dan again. They left the office, went through another room, into a corridor and down another stairway.

"After I found him at the desk," confessed Edgar, "I had to walk to the village and get the doctor. That was very brave of me. I don't like going out. Too many scary people out there."

As he said this, Frankie realized that *she* didn't feel scared of other people anymore. Maybe this was something she could help Edgar with too.

"Well, here we are." Edgar put the lamp down on a big oak table. Perry flew up and perched on top of a set of shelves. They were in a basement kitchen designed a hundred years ago for servants to prepare the household's meals. It had a big black wood-burning cook stove, deep enamel sinks, and pots hanging down from the ceiling. The windows were up high. Plants in the flowerbeds outside grew against the glass.

"I'll light the stove so we can cook something." Edgar opened a cupboard. It was full of cans. "What do you want — canned beans, canned spaghetti or canned chicken noodle soup?"

They decided on canned spaghetti with meatballs. When it was ready, Frankie dished up a bowl for Dan. He wolfed it down and promptly came to life again. He was so happy to be full he went galloping around the kitchen, then bent down with tail in the air to rub his whiskers on the floor.

"Hooray, Dan's better!" rejoiced Frankie. She rubbed her arms. "Now I just wish I could get warm."

Edgar looked at her in disbelief. "It's *hot* in here. Hmm. Maybe you're coming down with something." He went to get a tweed jacket hanging beside the door. "Here, put this on. It's great-grandpapa's."

"Thanks, Edgar."

"What're you doing here on that bike anyway?" Edgar asked. "What's it called again?"

"Hippogriff."

"I don't know what's so special about it," he said dismissively. "It's just a creaky old bike."

Frankie thought about that. Why didn't the bike work for Edgar? What had Augusta said? If you were confused and didn't know what you wanted, the bike just jammed up? Did that mean she, Frankie, was a clear-thinking person? Edgar sure seemed like a confused one.

"Augusta gave me the bike so I could come here to find her ring," Frankie explained. "She lost it in the lake at the Hotel Magnificat. And also she wanted me to get that envelope from Professor Proteus."

"Why did she send you? You're just a kid," said Edgar, getting up to put on the kettle for tea.

Frankie thought that was a bit much, coming from someone like Edgar. But she only said, "She's old and not very well. She said she needed someone special to find it. At first she said I was too young to go on my own, but she changed her mind when the social worker came to talk to me and my dad. Augusta said she needed to get me out of the way while she fixed everything." As she talked Frankie was fumbling in her knapsack for Dan's water dish. Her hand touched the wild hops that Dilly gathered for her. She remembered Dilly's words: if you made the hops into a tea, it would make you sleep. And Edgar was an insomniac.

"Do you want to try this tea, Edgar? It's supposed to make you sleep."

"Oh yes, anything, anything." Edgar beamed at her. Frankie stuffed the pot full of hops leaves and Edgar brought out a couple of mugs.

"This is so nice, isn't it?" Edgar said happily. "You and me here together. Why don't you just stay? We can cook together and you can read me stories and make sure everything runs smoothly. I'd be so happy to have someone to talk to."

"I can't, Edgar. I want to go home and see my dad and Augusta. I'm dying to show Augusta the ring." Frankie poured Edgar a cup of tea. "I just hope she's fixed up everything with dad and the social worker." Frankie put down the pot with a bang. "I've got it! What you need is a social worker!"

"I do?"

"Yes, you do, Edgar. A social worker will help you figure out how to pay your bills and to go out without being scared. That's what social workers do. They help people." Frankie was excited now. "They must have social workers here in Pigglestop. When I get home I'll tell the social worker about you and she can arrange things."

"If you say so, Francesca. I must say, this tea is having absolutely no effect on me. None at —" Edgar flopped down on the table, fast asleep. Perry the parrot flew down from the shelf, then sidled over to where Edgar's head lay cradled in his arms. Perry puffed out his feathers and leaned his head on Edgar's shoulder. Edgar murmured sleepily, "Good boy."

Frankie looked at Dan. "I thought he hated that parrot."

"What makes' say that?" Edgar slurred drowsily and started to snore.

"It's a miracle," thought Frankie sleepily, and before she knew it she was asleep too.

When Frankie woke up it was pitch black. She realized after a few seconds that Dan had woken her up. He was sitting at her feet, making a nearly silent whimper, staring at her in the dark, willing her awake. She didn't feel well and the room seemed to be swaying a bit. Suddenly, all she wanted to do was go home, right that instant.

"Edgar, wake up!" she urged. "I'm going home. Give me the key to the gate."

Edgar kept snoring.

"I guess he's really tired after not sleeping for three years," thought Frankie. "But how am I going to find my way out of here?" She was in the basement of a dark house that was like a maze. "I might as well be blind," she said aloud, and then she was reminded of the experiment in Augusta's bedroom.

You have powers of visualization and memory. That's what Augusta had said to her. But this place was much bigger than Augusta's room and Frankie had only seen it once by lamplight. She held her burning forehead in her hands, visualizing the kitchen. She reviewed the winding trip through the house, each staircase, hall and room in order, then in reverse. Then, when she felt she had it all in her head, she got off her chair, crouched down and felt for her knapsack. She slipped it over her shoulders, then slid along the edge of the table to Edgar.

"Edgar, wake up!" She shook his shoulder. Perry squawked sleepily, but not Edgar. He stayed resolutely in the land of dreams. Frankie crouched down to reach for Edgar's shirt pocket. The big skeleton key weighed his shirtfront down. She extracted the key, then straightened up and patted Edgar Proteus III on the shoulder.

"Don't forget to go to the bank to pay your bills tomorrow, Edgar. Then I can phone you about the social worker when I get back." Edgar murmured in his sleep. He sounded content.

Frankie and Dan began the long winding trek back through the house. Every so often, Frankie had to stop and rest her cheek against the cool wall and visualize the way again, but once they got upstairs her eyes became accustomed to the dark and she started to recognize the rooms they had passed through a few hours earlier. Dan was trotting behind her just like his old self. She opened the back door. The cool night air felt lovely on her hot face. She did up the buttons of Professor Proteus' tweed jacket, then crossed the cobblestones to the wall. Running her hands over the wood, she located the keyhole and unlocked and opened the door. Then she went back for the bike. When her fingers touched the handlebars she felt a golden warmth travel up her arms and spread through her body. It was as if Hippogriff was sending her a smile, welcoming her back. She wheeled the bike to the wall, picked up Dan and put him in the basket.

She made it as far as the edge of the clearing but there she had to stop. It was very dark in the woods and she felt feverish and dizzy. She got down off the seat and stood astride the bike. "Hippogriff," she whispered pleadingly. "I don't think I can ride." Then she said the words Mary had told her to say: *"Hippogriff, take me home."*

The Hippogriff ornament slowly began to turn, then spun faster as the bike changed configuration. Frankie found she was able to get up on the seat, lean on the handlebars and cradle her head in her arms. The bike rolled forward smoothly. Dan curled up in the basket and put his head down. They rolled down the hill through the forest. Frankie's feet were resting on the pedals, but the pedals didn't turn. Yet the bike went faster and faster, sailing down the road and sweeping smoothly along the curves. When they came to the river the bike simply sailed over it and onto the main road. Frankie fell into a feverish waking dream.

Sometimes she woke to see fields and farms roll by. Once a deer leapt across the road in front of her, its gleaming brown eye meeting hers in urgent sympathy.

Then the bear was driving a police car alongside them on the wrong side of the road and growling at them, and Zelda and Justin with the jewelry box were crammed into the back seat. The hotel owner leaned out the window and shouted, "Arrest that girl!"

Frankie's face was hot and sweaty and her heart pounded in terror of being caught. Then the car disappeared and they were sailing past a sweeping field of blowing grasses and stands of poplars. Atop a little rise, Dilly waved and jumped up and down. "See you in the movies, Frankie. Good luck good luck good luck!"

And then suddenly she was terrified to find herself on the freeway with the roar and wail of speeding cars and thundering trucks that rushed by in a suck of air and made the bike wobble in the downdraft. They were flying down the shoulder, blinded by headlights and blinking with the blobby afterimages of red and amber tail lights.

But the next time she woke they were sailing gently as a lullaby along a rolling country road that wound away for miles through the sleeping fields and farms. Above them a clear, dark midnight sky danced with glittering stars and a sliver of silver moon. It was so beautiful she was filled with rapture. The warm night air ruffled Dan's ears and he made a small, grumpy dog-dream bark.

They flew on, little knowing that gliding swiftly around the hills and past the farmyards came the silent black limousine of Zelda in pursuit.

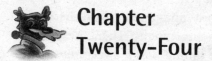 # Chapter
Twenty-Four

Ron got into bed at about one in the morning, having still heard nothing from the police in Pigglestop except they were still looking for Frankie. The police confirmed that Frankie had indeed been detained at the hotel but had managed to get away. So Ron knew she was fine as of that afternoon.

A little after 5:00 a.m., he gave up trying to sleep and turned on his clock radio:

"And in local news, a convicted child kidnapper on surpervised release in the Pigglestop area has failed to report in. Harold Rob Swindelson, otherwise known as The Crocodile, has made a career of kidnapping children and forcing them to work for him as thieves. Police are taking his disappearance very seriously. Parents are warned to be on the lookout for a tall man with prominent teeth and nose driving a brown Barracuda."

Ron sat up like a shot. "Oh my God! Frankie!" He threw on some clothes and ran for his car, "License or no license, I'm going!"

⌣·

Frankie and Dan woke up. They sat up. Frankie stretched while the bike resumed its usual shape. Her fever of last night was gone. She felt happy, refreshed and eager to get home. To see her dad and Germ and best of all, proudly hand Augusta the ring.

"We did it, Dan!" The air was crisp and fresh and every leaf and blade of grass glittered with dew in the early morning sunlight. Frankie took hold of Hippogriff's handlebars and pedalled.

"I recognize this!" she said wonderingly to Dan. They were getting very close to the edge of town and were almost at the spot where they had met the Bumbles. Frankie smiled. Mrs. Bumble would be surprised when she heard that her honey had saved her from a bear.

⌣·

The Crocodile drove along in his rumbling, dust-covered Barracuda. He switched off the news irritably. "Oh phooey! They've noticed I'm gone. Mr. Goody-Two-Shoes parole officer must have reported me. I'd better check in, otherwise I'll be back in jail before I can *recruit*," he giggled, "a single kid. I'd really like to catch that red-haired girl who did that amazing getaway on that old bike. Maybe she was an acrobat from the circus. That kind of talent would be really useful ... after a little brainwashing, that is."

The Crocodile ground his teeth. "Kids today are so honest. It's sickening." Complaining and muttering, he swept the houses on each side of the road with his carnivorous gaze as he drove along the rural road hoping for early risers. He came to the end of the road and turned onto the Old Highway wondering if he should just turn around and report to the parole office. Put on a tie. Say it's all been a big misunderstanding ... "Wait! There she is. All alone on that bike with that stupid dog in the basket." His torn knuckle whitened as he gripped the steering wheel angrily.

"Ooh, I HATE that dog! Well, she's not going to get away from me this time!" The Crocodile's face scrunched up, making his long nose stick out and his big nostrils flare. His wet teeth glistened in the morning sun as he taunted in a singsong voice, "Nobody's on the road. It's just you and me, Red."

Ron drove to the edge of town and took the turn for the Old Highway. He hadn't driven far when, off in the distance, he saw his little girl. She was riding towards him.

"There's Frankie!" he exclaimed. But in the next moment, his great flood of joy was replaced with pure terror. A car had pulled up beside her.

The Barracuda roared up alongside the bike. In their effort to avoid a collision, Frankie and Dan toppled over the guard rail and tumbled into the long grass on the other side. The bike was crushed between the car and rail. Frankie saw a man get out of his car, grinning a crocodile smile. She took off running. But the long-legged Crocodile was faster and grabbed her. Dan attacked and bit and wouldn't let go, but the man with the ugly heart was so angry he hardly noticed. Frankie went wild! She kicked and screamed. She bit his hairy wrist.

"Ow!" the Crocodile yelled, grunting and kicking at Dan. He grabbed Frankie with both hands and shook her hard. "Listen you. I prefer quiet little kids who do as they are told. But you'll just have to do."

Like a thunderbolt, a flash of gold and a clang came out of nowhere and the Crocodile dropped like he'd been shot. There stood Ron brandishing a very dented brass instrument. "I told you you're lucky your dad plays a euphonium," he said.

"Dad!"

Ron dropped to his knees and Frankie flew into his arms. Dan leapt and barked around them. Ron hugged Frankie very tight. They were both crying. He looked at her, "Honey, are you okay?" Frankie nodded.

"Okay, then. Let's dry up and look for something to tie this customer up with." They hurried over to Ron's car. It looked even stranger than usual. Ron rummaged under the front seat then popped back up. "Okay, I've got some upright bass strings. That should do the trick." He ran back and tied the ankles and wrists of the Crocodile, who was still out cold, then turned to Frankie. "Come on. Let's go home."

"Wait, Dad! The bike. It's hurt."

Ron eased the crumpled bike out from between the guard rail and the Crocodile's car and put it in his trunk. He and Frankie and Dan got into the car.

"Dad, why is your car full of musical instruments?"

Ron looked into the crammed back seat and laughed. "Bumpety bump bump." Frankie punched him. "Just kidding. Well, I was cleaning up the house and I ran out of room, so I thought I'd stick the stuff to be repaired into the car since I wasn't driving it. Speaking of which, I think I'll call the police anonymously about that crook back there. I'm not supposed to be driving." He turned to her, smiling hugely. "I'm so glad to see you, sweetheart. Your old dad was so worried. We've all been scared out of our wits — Augusta and Violet and the social worker."

"You talked to her, Dad?"

"Oh yeah. A lot. Things are going to —"

"Is she going to take me away?" Frankie's voice trembled.

"No, no, no, sweetie." Ron turned to her, his voice reassuring and gentle. "No, no, no. Everything's going to be alright. The social worker's on our side. She gave me a good scare to make me see the light, but ever since she's been helping me make a lot of changes so I can make a better home for us. Wait'll you see how clean it is. Violet helped me clean up the house and I've stopped drinking, and I got a new job as an assistant musical director, and joined a community band ..."

Frankie and Ron chatted so happily on the way home that neither noticed a black limousine purring behind them at a discreet distance.

Chapter
Twenty-Five

Frankie and Dan burst into Augusta's house, Dan barking and Frankie calling, "Augusta, Augusta. We're back. We got it! We got the ring!"

Augusta's relieved and triumphant voice called from the top of the stairs, "You're here! I knew you'd do it!"

Frankie and Dan hurled themselves onto the bed and into Augusta's arms. For once, she wasn't wearing a single ring.

"Child, child, are you alright? What happened to you? Mary called us in a panic. And the police are looking for you."

"I found her on the highway," Ron interrupted as he entered the room and joined them.

"Zelda locked me up," Frankie began to explain. She hardly knew where to start. "She said I was an international jewel thief."

"A what? She's obviously gone gaga. I, at least, still have all my faculties."

They could hear Violet starting up the stairs when the front door burst open. "Here, just a minute!" came Violet's protest. "You can't just come banging into a private home!"

"I have come to speak to my sister," said a voice accustomed to giving orders. "Where is she?"

"Zelda! I know that voice. Violet, don't let that monster in!" Augusta cried.

Zelda looked up the stairs. "Aha!" she snorted and started up.

Violet spread her arms wide and gripped a banister with each hand. Her face was determined. "Over my dead body, missus!"

Zelda grabbed one of Violet's thick wrists and tried to pull her hand off the banister, but Violet held firm. Zelda tried to duck under her arm, but before she could, Violet stuck out a leg. Furious, Zelda yelled up, "Augusta, you tell this woman to let me through this instant. I AM YOUR SISTER!"

"Oh, very well. But you behave yourself. I am surrounded by friends."

Zelda stormed into the room, shouldering Ron out of the way and exclaiming. "She was my mother, too! Why shouldn't I have the ring? You were Father's favourite just because you were the baby. But I remember Mother and I got nothing of hers."

Everyone was crowded in Augusta's bedroom now. Frankie and Dan were on the bed with Augusta. Ron and Violet, alarmed, stood watchful and ready to defend Augusta if things got out of hand.

"You! You monster! You cut off our father's finger!" Augusta accused shrilly.

"I did nothing of the kind! And I am *not* a monster! If you'd let me speak for once, I'll tell you what really happened."

"Very well, then." Augusta folded her arms. "Amaze me." Ron moved to the big armchair by the fireplace and Violet perched herself on the edge of a low bookcase. Zelda took a big breath.

"Late that night, after everyone had gone to bed, I crept down to the front parlour. I was leaning over the coffin trying to pull the ring off Father's finger when I heard someone coming. I ducked down beside the coffin so I couldn't be seen from the door, and I pulled father's hand with me. His little finger was resting just on the edge of the coffin. I was determined to get the ring off before I was discovered. One of the aunts came in. It was Maggie, the loopy one. She came into the room babbling away to Father, 'Are you getting a draft, Patrick? Shall I close the lid so you can have a good night's rest?' Well, then the silly old thing trips and falls against the coffin. She must have caught her nightgown on something. The lid slams down and the finger just dropped off into my lap — ring and all!"

Hearing this gruesome detail, Violet, Ron and Frankie all drew back. "Ew!" But Zelda and Augusta didn't notice. They were far into their past.

"So then she's twittering and apologizing to Father and the other aunt yells from the other room, 'For God's sake, Maggie, go to bed!' So she did. She never saw me or knew what she'd done."

"I don't believe it, "Augusta gasped. "I am simply flabbergasted, Zelda. For God's sake, why didn't you tell them?"

"Because, idiot! They would have wanted the finger back and the ring was still stuck!"

"Francesca." Augusta turned to her. "Did you find Father's finger?"

"Augusta, try not to be a dolt," Zelda answered for her. "It's been sixty years! It decomposed, or some fish ate it and got terrible indigestion."

"Don't be disgusting. You're talking about our father." Augusta had another thought, "But I thought you were going to sell the ring to industry and make a killing."

"Oh, I was never going to do that. I was just trying to drive you crazy. You already believed I was a monster. Besides I've already made a killing in the hotel business."

"But you remember Mother," Augusta's imperious voice suddenly became very sad and small. "I don't remember her at all. The ring is all I have. You at least knew her. Had her to yourself until I was born."

Frankie started to say something but Ron put his finger to his lips and beckoned for her to come. She slid off the bed and went to him. He pulled her up onto his lap and put his arms around her. "They need to talk," he whispered in her ear.

Frankie was amazed to hear two elderly sisters fighting over their mother's love as if they were children. She suddenly saw the two little girls from the sepia photographs inside of each sister, still alive and kicking, angry, playful, or hurt, and in need of consoling. Both still with an ache for a mother gone too soon.

"The letter from Professor Proteus," Frankie suddenly remembered. She pulled the crumpled envelope out of her bib pocket. Ron looked at it. "It's for you, Augusta."

"Would you do the honours, Ron?"

Zelda turned, indignant to see someone else in the room. "Who's he when he's at home?"

Mildly, Ron introduced himself. "Ron Rudderless, Francesca's father. You know, the international jewel thief?" Zelda glared at him. Ron couldn't help looking a little smug as he opened the letter. Frankie gently punched him. Ron began to read:

My Dearest Augusta,

As your godfather, it has always grieved me that you and Zelda were unable to reconcile your differences. You are each so like your parents. If only you could be friends you might have recovered from the tragic early loss of your parents and found comfort in being together. I can only pray that this might still happen after I am gone, although it would have given me great joy to see it in my lifetime.

As you know, your father and I worked for many years on human responsive metals, but we abandoned our research after the apparent failure of the Hippogriff prototype. As well, I just didn't have the heart to continue after your father died. I went on with other research. But recently, in my retirement, I have again started to think about the work we did. I got out my notes and discovered a small sample of modified metal that remained. It was the very same gold that your mother's ring, a sentimental gift at the time, was made of.

We thought at first that the metal was so responsive that it would immediately realign itself to any human it touched, thereby losing the record of the previous contact. What I have found since, though, is that the first wearer's "signature" remains like a ghost that can be reactivated and strengthened should the metal encounter the same human imprint again. But a stranger would FEEL NOTHING AT ALL BECAUSE THE RING MUST ENCOUNTER THE ORIGINAL HUMAN ESSENCE IN ORDER TO MAGNIFY IT.

Augusta, you and Zelda need never have fought over this ring. Each of you contains the imprint of your mother in your genes, or DNA. *Any time either of you wears it, the "ghost" of your mother's electron pattern that the ring still holds will reverberate to the essence of your mother that is in each of you. Furthermore, as you are siblings, each of you has aspects of your mother that the other does not and sharing the ring will fill in the patterning to virtual completion.*

Much love to you, my dear,
Your loving Uncle Curious

Frankie slid off Ron's lap and knelt beside Dan. She felt for his collar fastening, pressed the release and slipped off the ring. She stood up and walked over to the bed where Zelda was still standing next to Augusta.

"Here it is." She opened her hand. The ring glittered in her palm. Everyone held their breath. Zelda picked up the ring then passed it to her sister.

"Go on Augusta, you first. The child found it for you."

"No, no, you go first, Zelda."

"I couldn't, you do it, Augusta."

"Blimey! Will somebody put the blinkin' thing on! The suspense is killing me!" exclaimed Violet.

Zelda slid the ring onto her little finger. Everyone stared. Then, before their eyes, Zelda visibly relaxed. You could see the iron leave her shoulders and her jaw. The rigidity flowed out of her body. She looked younger and happier. She laughed. "Oh Oggie, it's mother. It's wonderful. Here, you try."

Augusta's hands trembled as she took the ring and slid it on. It fit perfectly. "I don't believe it. I don't believe it." Tears leaked out from under her dark glasses. She held the cameo to her withered cheek. "My dear mama. My poor dear mama."

Watching her, Zelda began to cry noisily.

"Come here, Zee." Augusta held out her arms.

Zelda knelt and buried her face in her sister's neck — the younger consoling the elder. "Oh, Oggie. I'm so sorry," came her muffled voice.

"I know, I know. I am too."

After a bit, Zelda sat up to blow her nose. "You know Og," (honk), "you look exactly like mother."

"I do?" Augusta sounded delighted. "Well, I've never told you this, but I always thought you looked exactly like Daddy."

"Really?" Zelda was enchanted. "Well, bless your cotton socks for saying so, you dear girl."

And they went on in this vein until Mrs. Slatternly asked them what they wanted to do about breakfast.

But during all this, Ron was frowning. Something was niggling at him. Suddenly it came to him.

"Frankie, could you help Violet set the table and get the tea ready?" he asked. Zelda was on the phone ordering a buffet breakfast in from the Grand Hotel. ("I'm an owner. We do a fabulous brunch.")

When Frankie was busy, Ron sidled up to Augusta and whispered. "Augusta, do you remember that little ring you lent to Cally and me when we were too broke to buy a wedding ring? It wasn't — "

"Oh, you clever man! I'd completely forgotten. Yes it was. It most certainly was."

Brunch was indeed fabulous. They all sat at the table for hours laughing and talking.

Frankie recounted every detail of her adventure from the beginning to the end. The others relived every moment, and in her mind's eye Augusta saw everything.

"Francesca, my little fox, my special soul. You remarkable thing, you! Just how many fairy godmothers were there around your cradle?"

～

That night, Ron tucked Frankie in.

"Comfy?"

Frankie nodded happily.

"Okay, I'm going to tell you a story. A long time ago, oh I'd say over ten years ago, there was a boy and a girl who were very much in love. The girl's name was Cally and the boy's name was Ron. They wanted to get married, but they were very poor. So a kind old lady lent them a plain little ring. It was so skinny it was hardly there at all. 'Just until you can afford something better,' the old lady told them." Frankie's ears tingled. "So they got married and the girl wore the little ring for a whole year, and during that year she was very happy. But the marriage didn't work out in the end, and when it was over the plain little ring was put in a box, and everyone forgot about it until today." Ron reached into his pocket. "And here it is." He put it into Frankie's hand, then he kissed her. He went to the door and turned out the light, "Night, baby."

Frankie put on the ring then lay back on her pillow, closed her eyes, and waited.

"Mommy!" she whispered. Then, smiling, she curled up under the covers and went to sleep.

From then on, Frankie had three fairy godmothers. She and Augusta and Violet spend every summer with Zelda at the Hotel Magnificat. Mary often joins them, and Ron comes on weekends and when he gets time off from his new job as music-program director of the city's community bands. Marisa the social worker is thrilled with his continued success and has declared him a model father and her best client ever. She also got Edgar out of the house and enrolled in a life-skills program. ("He's not bad really, just a little mad.") The man with the crocodile smile is doing very well in the prison pottery program. He says he repents, but nobody believes him so it's a good thing he's enjoying the pottery.

Most days, Augusta, looking aristocratic and glamorous in a gauzy scarf and sunglasses, sits on the terrace of the hotel with her friend and companion, Mrs. Violet Slatternly. They take tea in the mornings and sherry in the late afternoon. And often in the balmy evenings after dinner, Frankie and Ron serenade them with duets.

And yes, Frankie did see the Sharmskys at their next family reunion and has been to every family reunion since.

Acknowledgements

I would like to thank Joy Gugeler for digging my manuscript out of the slush pile and championing it. I am happily indebted to Lynn Henry for her thoughtful, perceptive, ever-courteous editing and tactful instruction on how to write a novel. I could not have written this book without her.

I would also like to thank Megan Johnstone for being an articulate ten-year-old; CWILL British Columbia for professional support; and friends Norma Larson, Paul Krampitz and Ross Waddell for their enthusiastic help with knotty plot problems.

About the Author

Cynthia Nugent is a lifelong closet writer and compulsive diarist. She is also a visual artist and illustrator of acclaimed picture books such as *Mister Got-to-Go*, *Mister Got-to-Go and Arnie* and *Goodness Gracious, Gulliver Mulligan*.

Cynthia lives in Vancouver with her Yorkshire Terrier Emma, and plays trumpet in a community band. This is her first novel.